I0572632

Other books by Charles Brownson
Ancestors (Jump River Press, 1984
In Uz (Noumenon Press, 1985)
The Figure of the Detective (McFarland, 2013)
from Ocotillo Arts
E (omnibus edition)
The Expatriate
Stories from The Book of Ka
The Ishtar Stories
Lullaby
Now the Artists Book Now
Out There
Paris 1953 Walking Tour
Twenty-Two Remarks on the Old Ones
The Way of the Tree
The Yuma Project

AS TOLD TO

a detective story

by

CHARLES BROWNSON

Tell me a story

The conversation

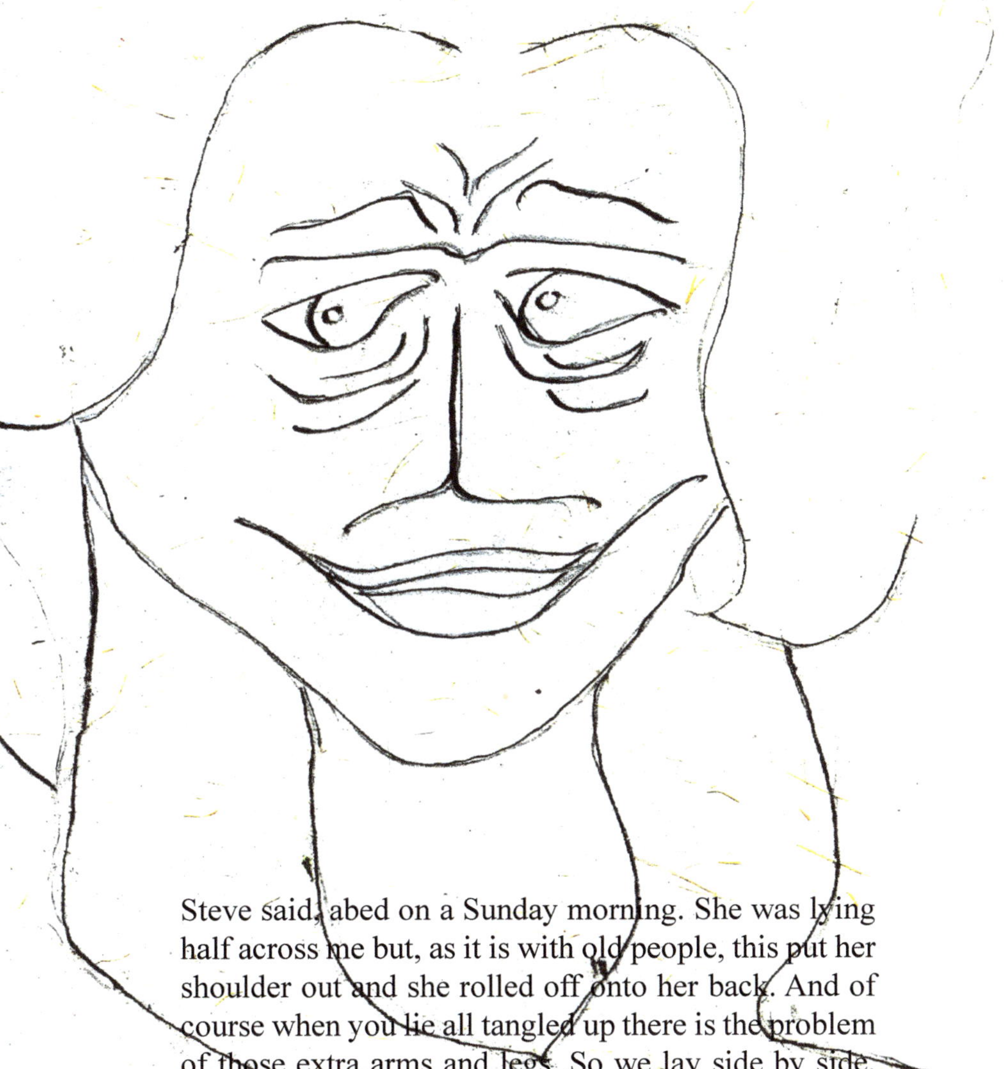

Steve said, abed on a Sunday morning. She was lying half across me but, as it is with old people, this put her shoulder out and she rolled off onto her back. And of course when you lie all tangled up there is the problem of those extra arms and legs. So we lay side by side, hands folded on our stomachs, naked as two corpses, and I said

What sort of story?

A short one. I'm getting hungry.

I could bring you a scrambled egg.

And coffee. Yum.

But no, Steve said, before I could bestir myself. Story first.

Very well. A couple –

Men? Women?

A man and a woman are sitting at a sidewalk table at a café in Paris.

Is it springtime?

No. That's hackneyed. Let's say Vienna. The Café Sperl.

There are no sidewalk tables at the Sperl. There's no sidewalk, as I remember.

OK, Paris. It's past the season. A little rainy. In a few days the waiters will fold up the umbrellas. It's morning. Early, I think. There's a couple of saucers on the table.

So they've been there a while. I'll bet they're cold.

There's a half-eaten brioche.

Cold.

Yes. They're wearing identical black leather jackets, and they've put their heads together. They could be twins.

They're not twins.

No.

What are they saying?

I don't know, do I? They're talking so quietly even the waiter can't hear. The woman fishes in the pocket of her jacket and puts ten francs on the table.

Francs. This was some time ago, then.

After the war.

Ten francs was a lot, then.

Was it? Well, she wants the waiter to stop hanging around, I suppose. He's in his shirtsleeves. With those armbands to keep his cuffs from getting into things.

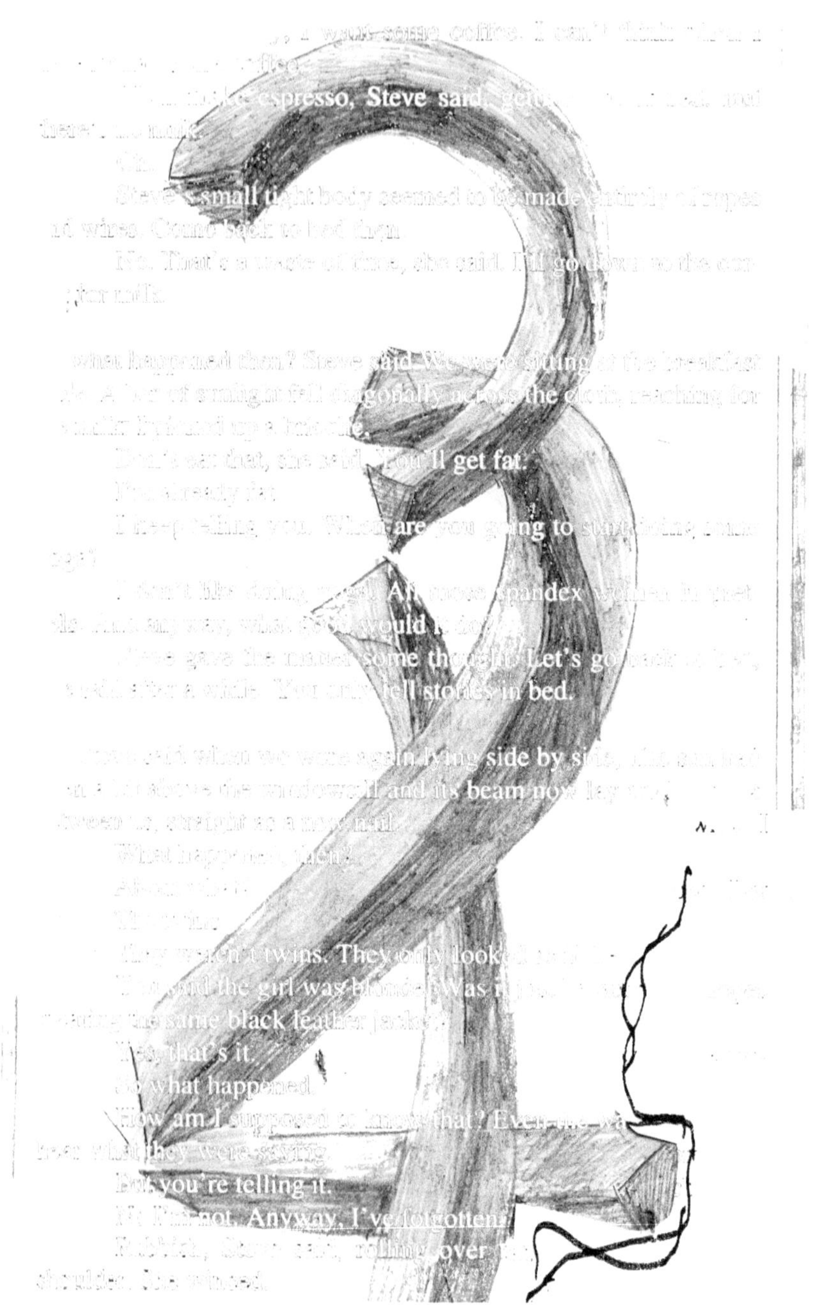

..., I want some coffee. I can't think without ... coffee.

... make espresso, Steve said, get ... back, and there's ... milk.

Oh.

Steve's small tight body seemed to be made entirely of ropes and wires. Come back to bed then.

No. That's a waste of time, she said. I'll go down to the corner for milk.

What happened then? Steve said. We were sitting at the breakfast ... A bar of sunlight fell diagonally across the cloth, reaching for ... he picked up a brioche.

Don't eat that, she said. You'll get fat.

I'm already fat.

I keep telling you. When are you going to start doing some ...?

I don't like doing that. All those spandex women in spot ... And anyway, what good would it do?

Steve gave the matter some thought. Let's go back to bed for a while. You only tell stories in bed.

She said when we were again lying side by side, the sun had risen above the windowsill and its beam now lay ... between us, straight as a new nail.

What happened then?

About ...

They ...

They weren't twins. They only looked ... and the girl was blonde. Was ... wearing the same black leather jacket ...

Yes, that's it.

So what happened.

How am I supposed to know that? Even the ... never what they were saying.

But you're telling it.

I'm not. Anyway, I've forgotten.

Bullshit, Steve said, rolling over ... shoulder. She winced.

He's eavesdropping.

Yes.

This is an awful slow story.

You keep interrupting.

Well, you're leaving things out.

Say, who's telling this story?

So, then, I said after stopping to think, the red-haired girl –

There's another girl?

A boy.

Is he red-haired?

 Swarthy.

I thought you said they were twins.

Could be, was what I said.

Hmm, Steve said, looking up at the ceiling. I think there's a continuity problem here. There was a big cobweb in the corner by the window.

Pipe down, I said. Anyway, I want some coffee. I can't think when I haven't had some coffee.

We'll have espresso, Steve said, getting out of bed. But there's no milk.

Oh.

Steve's small tight body seemed to be made entirely of ropes and wires. Come back to bed, then.

No. That's a waste of time, she said. I'll go down to the corner for milk.

So what happened then? Steve said. We were sitting at the breakfast table. A bar of sunlight fell diagonally across the cloth, reaching for the milk. I picked up a brioche.

Don't eat that, she said. You'll get fat.

I'm already fat.

I keep telling you. When are you going to start doing some yoga?

I don't like doing yoga. All those spandex women in pretzels. And anyway, what good would it do?

Steve gave the matter some thought. Let's go back to bed, she said after a while. You only tell stories in bed.

So, Steve said when we were again lying side by side. The sun had risen a bit above the windowsill and its beam now lay on the duvet between us, straight as a new nail.

What happened, then?

About what?

The twins.

They weren't twins. I've decided against the twins business.

So what happened.

How am I supposed to know that? Even the waiter couldn't hear what they were saying.

But you're telling it.

No I'm not. Anyway, I've forgotten.

Rubbish, Steve said, rolling over to lay her head on my shoulder, She winced.

What happened was, Steve said, the red-haired girl stood up, knocking the saucers and the half-eaten brioche and the ten francs to the sidewalk, and gave the dark-haired boy a slap on the face. It cracked like lightning. The waiter took a step back, stumbled on the curb, and fell down. His tray went swirling into the street.

I suppose he tore a hole in his pants then. The waiter.

Hush. The boy pushed his chair over and stood up, his face as red as his hair.

I thought he had black hair, I said.

Hush, Steve said. The girl turned, pulled a gun from under her jacket, and shot the waiter in the head.

What? Why?

How do I know, she said. Who's telling this story?

I WAS THINKING, I said, totally disrupting the Monday morning routine, about that story you told me yesterday.

I didn't tell it, Steve said obstinately.

We did, then.

Whatever.

What I want to know is –

How's it going to end.

No. I already know that.

How do you know that, Steve asked, for once genuinely interested.

Because I'm telling the story.

No you're not.

Whatever. What I want to know is, why did she slap the boy?

Steve considered. We ought to begin, she began, at the beginning, to work out who the boy is. Not her twin, you said. Her brother, then.

Good, I agreed. They *are* a lot alike.

Except in every respect but the leather jackets.

Never mind, I said, nettled, to cut this argument short. Brother. No twins.

Let's wait and see, I said. If one shows up.

Say on, Horatio.

Rosalind. Wrong play. Do you not know I am a woman?

Are you?

No, that's what Rosalind… never mind.

Steve angrily broke her toast in half, scattering buttered crumbs everywhere and presaging events to come.

So, I said. The boy.

Questions pour down like rain. Who *are* these mugs? What were they trying to accomplish? And why was Jack in such a hurry? And what difference does it make where they started from? I had a hunch that, before this was over, I'd be sorry I asked.

That's Tracer Bullet. Watterson's P.I. He's not in this story.

He would be, if Watterson weren't so particular with his permissions.

Steve, can we just get on with this?

OK. So the crime and the criminal are pretty obvious. The Chronicler is us. Who are the threatened bystanders?

Is this an English Classic?

Neo-Classic. No one writes the old ones anymore. OK, so we'll skip the bystanders for the time being. The Detective.

Well, I said. There isn't much room for one, is there?

How about a lawyer? Steve suggested. She's going to need a lawyer. He needs to prove it's a *crime passionelle* or something. The lawyer could bring in a P.I. to work that out. Go backwards and forwards. Clean up the spilled milk.

That's Oliver Lacan, in the Smiley trilogy.

Is it? Never mind, let's go with it.

I don't believe it, said Monsieur Delarue to his clerk Dehanty. And neither will the Investigating Magistrate.

She is lying, Monsieur?

No, I think not. I doubt if she is a good liar in any case. Liars don't pop up and shoot waiters in public for no apparent reason.

She is, ah… hiding the truth, then

Something like that, Dehanty. Something like that.

Unfortunate, Dehanty said quietly. His first name was Robert, but Monsieur Delarue never used it. They were all quite formal here. As for *tu,* after forty years of association that was unimaginable. Dehanty was now almost sixty, and Delarue only a few years older. Neither of them had ever married or tutoyered anyone.

Unfortunate for whom? Delarue replied sharply. It is unacceptable in any case, aside from the Magistrate's making me out to be a fool. It will be Gauthier. Merciless man. We must take steps.

Dehanty after long experience said nothing. Delarue sat at his desk bouncing a pencil on its eraser. Dehanty had never seen this pencil used for any other purpose. To his knowledge it had been sharpened only once, years ago, upon the decease of its predecessor, which had lost the resilience of its eraser. Monsieur Delarue used a fountain pen, one with rust-colored ink. Dehanty hadn't the patience to write anything by hand and had used a typewriter since 1943, among lawyers a very unpopular thing to do.

Villainous, Monsieur pronounced upon the first pages printed from this word processor, and dropped them into the wastebasket under the impression he was destroying something. After that, Dehanty transcribed his typewriting in an acid green ink, judiciously redacting it to save work, and filed the other copy for himself.

Enfin, Monsieur said now. We must look into this. There are several points. Who was the waiter? She says that he was an Egyptian spy. Patently ridiculous. Daft, even.

A Palestinian Jew, wasn't he? So the Inspector said.

As Told To

Tell me a story, Steve said, in bed on a Sunday morning. She was lying half across me but, as it is with old people, this put her shoulder out and she rolled off onto her back. And of course when you lie all tangled up there is the problem of those extra arms and legs. So we lay side by side, hands folded on our stomachs, naked as two corpses, and I said

What sort of story?

A short one. I'm getting hungry.

I could bring you a scrambled egg.

And coffee. Yum.

But no, Steve said, before I could bestir myself. Story first.

Very well.

A couple...

Men? Women?

A man and a woman are sitting at a sidewalk table at a café in Paris.

Is it springtime?

No. That's hackneyed. Let's say Vienna. The Café Sperl.

There are no sidewalk tables at the Sperl. There's no sidewalk, as I remember.

Exactly. And what was he so curious about, this Jew? Which is to say, what does *Madame* have to hide? Or rather, what can a woman such as she – red hair, leather airman's jacket, tattoos (conventional, we're told, among her ilk), atrocious French – possibly be capable of hiding?

An American expatriate, Dehanty observed. Why do these people live so squalidly when they can afford better? Not the rue Balzac, of course, but that pissoir on the rue de la Hachette?

Across from the Noctambules?

Monsieur, *non.* Le Théâtre de la Huchette. Number 23.

Ah, stupid of me. Where they have played *La Cantatrice Chauve* seemingly since the deluge.

Since 1950, Monsieur.

Is it? Two years? *Ainsi,* Madame lives below her means, with a person passed off as her brother –

I believe, Monsieur, he really is her brother. The Inspector –

Oh, là là, cet *Inspecteur.* Very well, Dehanty. You are right. Her brother. But that was a lover's slap, I insist.

Very well. But I must point out that Madame has only $100 a month. She is hardly living below her means.

Tut tut, Dehanty. Rodolphe says it is possible to live well on twenty sous.

Monsieur, that was in 1840, and said of a squalid life among the most abject of criminals.

Wait a minute, Steve interrupted at this point. He knows nothing at this point, your *avocat*. Witnesses have not been questioned. There *were* no witnesses. It was late in the season, the café was empty. This is all conjecture and irrelevancies from old novels.

They were sitting on the street, I temporized. There must have been witnesses.

Well, it wasn't the Boul' Miche, was it? It was a side street off the rue Mouffetard. There was no one on the street. So how does Monsieur Delarue know that it was a lovers' slap?

All right, we'll take that out. Anyway, if he is to be a brother I don't think we ought to muck about with a slap of that sort.

Certainly not, Steve said, firmly certain. Far too complicating.

By the way, I said, when did we decide on the rue Mouffetard?

Hemingway lived there.

Did he? What's that got to do with it?

Nothing, she said serenely.

What happened was, Steve said, th
knocking the saucers and the half-eaten bri
to the sidewalk, and gave the dark-haired bspar ex women in pret-
cra like lightning. The waiter took a ste
c and fell down. His tray went sailing inh go back to
I suppose he tore a hole in his pants in
Hush. The boy pushed his chair c
So, Steve said when we were again lying side
risen a bit above the windowsill and its beam no
between us, straight as a new nail.
What happened, then?
About what?

A cup of café au lait sat on Gaspard Delarue's desk. It had now gone cold; nevertheless, he drank what was left, making a face. Dehanty offered to refill it but was waved away. A shaft of sunlight straight as a nail fell across the desktop from the window which had not been washed since before the war. Due to a gap in the roof of the building across the alley, this bar of sunlight would last only five minutes, reaching across the Boulevard de Sébastopol at exactly 10 am in winter, provided, of course, it was not raining.

What could they have been talking about, I wonder, said Monsieur Delarue quietly, as to himself. He raised his head with its theatrical white hair and magnificent clear walnut eyes. Look into that, Dehanty. See what you can find out about these people. You can get into that hôtel where they are all living without being much noticed. (Dehanty opened his eyes at that.) Question the conciêrge. Where does their money come from? Spy or no spy, I would wager there is some connection with the American war presence, even if it is only the Red Cross. The United Nations, probably. Attaché of some sort. Everyone is an attaché.

Well, Monsieur Delarue, perhaps not women with tattoos who wear black leather jackets and carry guns.

Hmm. These tattoos. There are several? Visible?

I believe so. On her arms. There was something about her décolleté…

Delicate of you, Dehanty. I don't want to hear about it.

No, monsieur.

What do they do? Sit around in cafés? Surely not.

There is a magazine of some sort, I believe.

Writers, Delarue said scornfully. Worse: poets.

Publishers, I believe.

What? In French?

English.

Ah. One of those.

Oui, monsieur. *Ceux-là.*

Well, said Delarue with distaste, see to it then, Dehanty. Let us confer here after dinner. Nine o'clock.

I will see what I can do, monsieur.

Bien.

Dehanty In Hell

The day being still fine, with a high blue sky, Dehanty decided to walk to the rue de la Hachette. He put on a leather dress coat and wrapped a tartan wool scarf around his neck. Emerging into the street, he walked briskly toward the river, crossed over to the Left Bank by the Île de la cité and the Petit pont, and a block farther turned right into the rue de la Hachette. At this point his steps slowed.

But, despite this reluctance, he arrived eventually at the door which, when opened, confirmed his expectations. Inside, in a dark foyer no more than a meter square, were the bottom steps of a worn and rickety-looking stair, and opposite the concièrge's window. The air was thickened by an indefinable reek composed of cabbage and unfamiliar spices along with a rotting fish smell dating probably from Roman times. The concièrge's window flew up. The concièrge herself was, to Dehanty's surprise, a young woman, well-spoken, making one concession to the *rôle* with a cigarette, rolled herself, stuck to her lower lip, and a second concession, Dehanty found as he approached the window, which was to keep a cat.

Here was the origin of the spicy smell. The cabbages were illegally stewing somewhere above, probably on a campfire on the floor. Dehanty inquired after Constanza Lee.

Not here, said the concièrge in a voice decidedly contradicting her appearance. Arrested. She peered at Dehanty through a cloud of tobacco smoke as if he might be another of the johns responsible for Mademoiselle Lee's downfall.

Her brother, then? Caswell is his name, I believe.

Four, she said with a sneer and slammed down the window.

Dehanty climbed up the stairs into an ever thicker fug. On each succeeding floor the rooms became smaller, and on four, below the garret, there was only one of these closet-sized rooms per apartment, as he found when the first was opened at his knock.

Monsieur Lee, please, he said to the shirtless Algerian in the doorway.

The Algerian indicated with a jerk of his head a room farther down the hall.

SHLOP
SHLOP
SHLOP

There were several of these. No one answered when Dehanty knocked at the first two. He had fastidiously put on his leather gloves before coming in, but still recoiled at the need to touch anything, and his knocking was rather delicate. There was a good deal of boisterous noise here. He imagined the Lees and all their expatriate American friends living in one room, with perhaps a corner or two sublet to some Serbian porters, squashed together probably half-naked.

And indeed, the woman who opened on his third knock seemed to be in her chemise. This garment, he later learned, was a *t-shirt*.

Not here, she said in response to his inquiry. Out. Her French was intelligible though marred by a peculiar accent. Come in, she offered, and Dehanty sidled through the opening.

Within there were only this woman and a man, lying on the sagging bed reading an English book. He took no notice of Dehanty. On a table stood a spirit stove with a pot of water waiting to be boiled, perhaps for coffee. The whole building was unheated, and here on the uppermost floor it was bitterly cold, yet nobody seemed to care.

The woman to whom he was speaking had a tattoo splayed across her collarbone, reaching down onto the upper curve of her breasts, an elaborate bird.

Who are you? she asked, but not unfriendly.

The room did have a window, but little light came through. The walls were a scabrous brown the color of mud. *Boue.* The window-sill was rotten and the spicy smell of the street floor had turned up here to urine.

My name is Dehanty, he said. I am clerk to Monsieur Delarue –

Oh yes. Con's lawyer.

Mademoiselle Constanza.

Oui, she said with amusement. Con.

She has a brother, I believe.

Cas.

I was hoping to speak to him.

Try the bistro on the corner. It's too damned cold to stay here.

Dehanty understood that this couple had remained behind for business of their own and quickly retired, leaving behind a small bow. The door shut, knocking his hat askew. Regaining the street

and the sunshine, he took a deep breath. Carefully he removed his gloves, folded them inside a handkerchief, and put them into a pocket of his coat. Looking toward each end of the rue he discovered the bistro where Constanza's brother was supposed to be, only a few steps away on his right. At that end of the rue was a small *place* formed by the intersection of three streets at an angle, with a single bench in the enclosed triangle. The bistro stood here, looking toward the Seine not far off. Dehanty went in.

There was no one in the bistro who could have been Caswell Lee, only a young woman by herself and two old men, neighborhood cronies at a guess. Dehanty asked the counterman, giving him the best description he could, but somehow gave the wrong impression of his intentions and the counterman only shrugged. An artificial gesture, a contemptuous *gallic* shrug. Perhaps he wanted money. Offended, Dehanty turned his back.

On the street again, he decided to walk down to the café where the shooting had happened. This proved to be on a another little triangular cobbled *place* with a miniature fountain in the middle. The café was on the short side of the triangle between the two streets, one of which ended here and the other continued on to join the rue Mouffetard.

Here again he began unhelpfully. The proprietor seemed to think Dehanty was some préfecture official come to threaten him about his license. He acknowledged the facts concerning his dead waiter, confirming what Dehanty already knew, and would add nothing about who the waiter was, who had recommended him, or anything about his behavior.

"No, monsieur" and "Who can say?" and that *shrug* were his whole repertoire of denials. Meanwhile, he was wiping his hands continuously on his dirty white apron. The apron's tie tunneled under his belly. He had the shoes of a man all day on his feet, seven days a week from five in the morning to late at night. And now he was short his waiter and his time was being taken up by threatening officials and suspicious policemen. He wiped his hand across his balding head, leaving a streak of tomato sauce which had somehow escaped the apron.

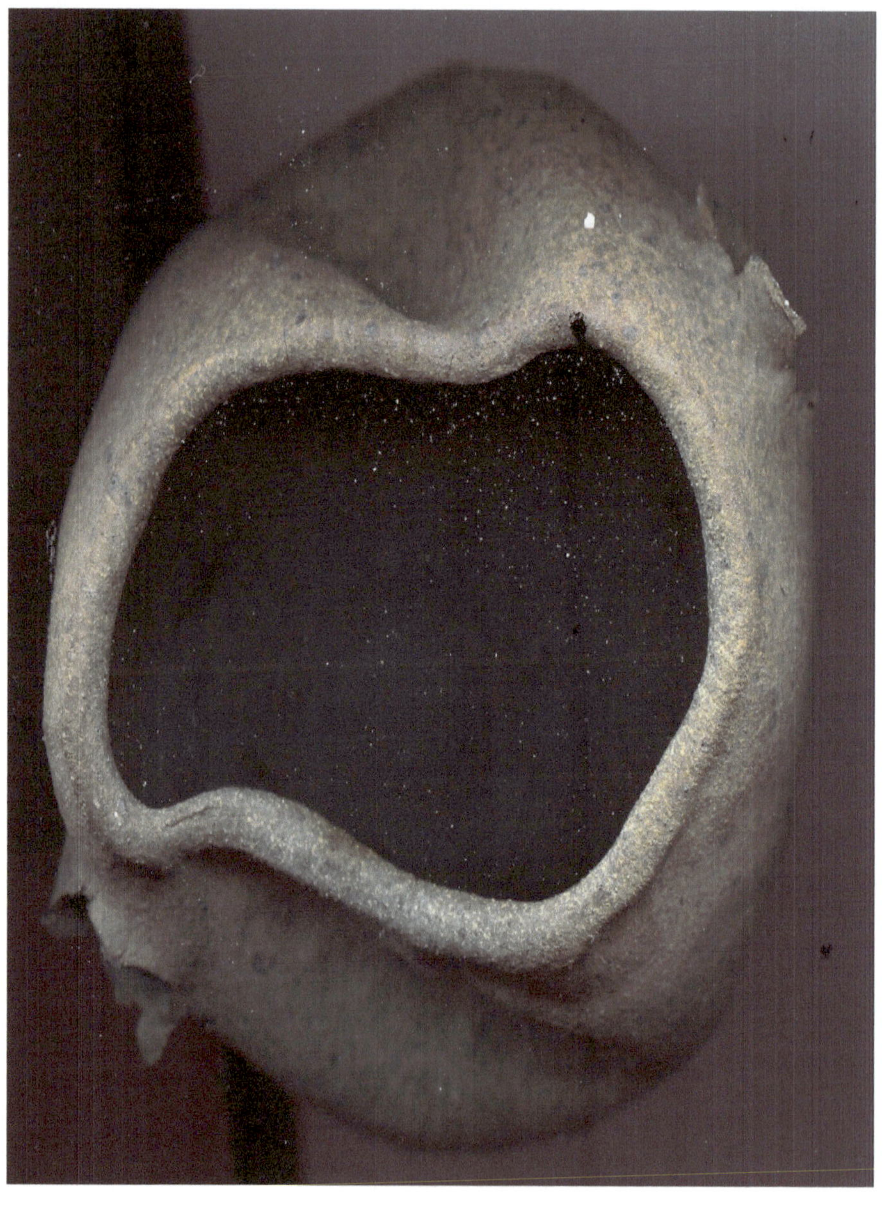

All Dehanty found out was the address of the room in which the waiter had been living. This proved to be in another hôtel like the first, also on the fourth floor, and the man who answered Dehanty's soft gloved knock might have been the very same shirtless Algerian of the Hachette.

This was a decent place, Dehanty thought, again on the street. They waited until he was dead to rent out his room again.

Where do Jewish waiters from Palestine and leather jacketed poets from America spend their time off? Dehanty wondered.

In *les caves*, the old wine cellars and sub-basements converted to jazz nightclubs after the war. Their first unregulated days had been as heady as a naked black dancer covered by a banana in this otherwise jaded city, but the craze burned off when the government asked for its share and now t *les caves* were now no more than ordinary dives.

Dehanty thought he might drop into one of these on his way back to report to Monsieur Delarue, and perhaps find something to eat, humble and inexpensive, with a glass of house wine.

At last matters fell in with desires – he found instead a small restaurant near the Pont Saint-Michel where he got a large bowl of onion soup and two glasses of decent red wine. A more congenial place, the waiter gave him directions to a couple of well-known *caveux*The entrance of the first one, Dehanty found, was somewhat indirect, as might be expected for the service entrance of an old cellar. It was early. The place was desultory now; it would come to life in the smaller hours. Dehanty asked for a glass of calvados and settled into an obscure corner, hunched within his fine black leather coat with his gloves in his pocket.

The musicians had abandoned the stage until the audience were larger. A bar girl came by and sat down, which made Dehanty squirm, but he bought her a brandy anyway. She was talkative. Real work would not begin for a couple of hours; she had time on her hands. The death of Monsieur Ammar was on her mind. As it was, she said, on the minds of waiters and bar girls and everyone else here who now thought what had been unimaginable before, that someone unknown, some stranger in the crowd, might stand up and inexplicable shoot a gun at them. A gun? Who walks around with a gun in their pocket?

Purse, I believe, in this case, said Dehanty, who valued exactness. Was that his name, then? Ammar? I suppose that was his, er – not a Christian name… His family name?

No one knows, monsieur. That is how everyone is called. Perhaps in Algeria it is a name like – she searched her mind – *John Doe* – en? Could I have another brandy?

So much for the Palestinian Jew, Dehanty thought with chagrin, and bought the second brandy with a little less reluctance.

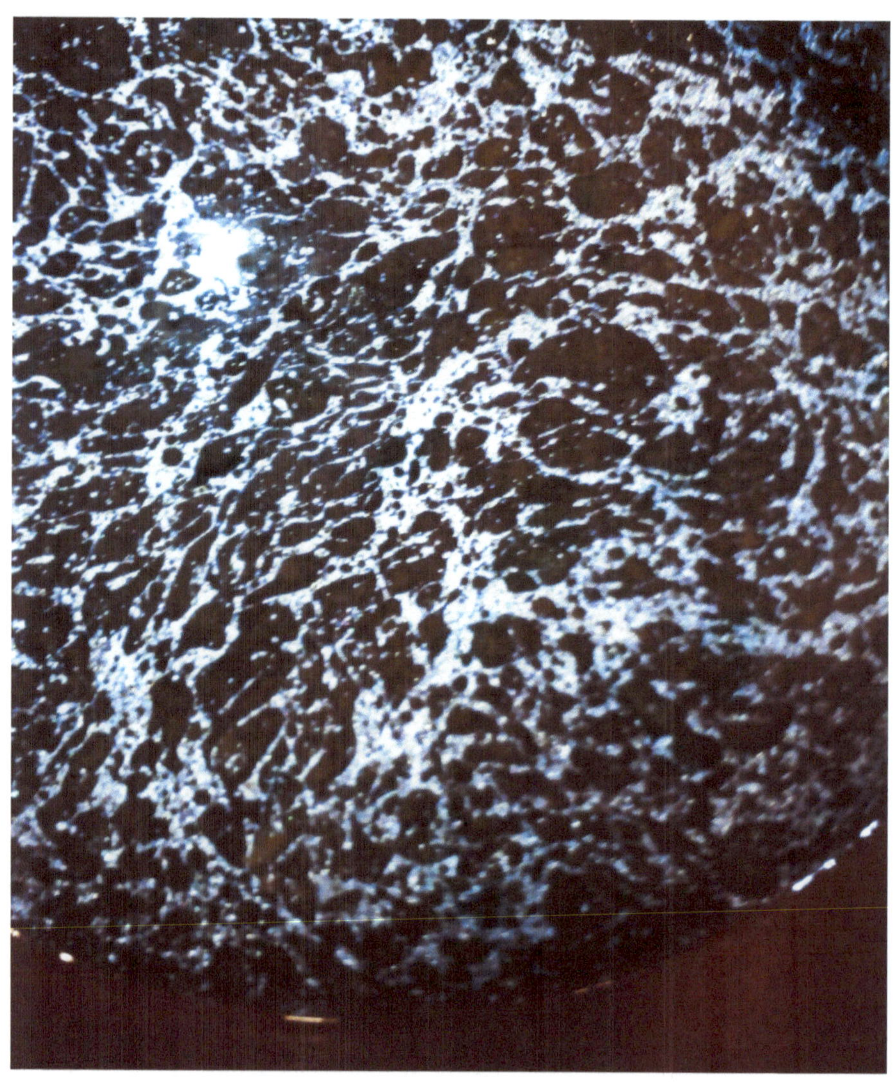

You've gone and made a continuity mistake, Steve said. We agreed that Mademoiselle Constanza –

Madame. Nobody says *mademoiselle* anymore.

They did in 1952. We agreed that Constanza was to have flaming red hair and a distinctive tattoo. Constanza is now in the pokey. Who is this woman delicto in Caswell's room? And if that's her brother, who is supposed to be downstairs in the bistro, we are going to have to revise that slap again, too.

It will work itself out, I said.

In stories like this things do not work *themselves* out. They have to be encouraged. The strappado and the rack.

That afternoon, I went on, Dehanty spent his time looking into the magazine which *Mademoiselle* Lee and her friends were said to be publishing. A few inquiries in some French and English bookshops specializing in the sort of magazine he assumed it to be confirmed that it published fiction and poetry of an avant-garde sort. It was entitled *Brown Paper Wrapper*, appeared at irregular intervals – presumably whenever enough money was found to pay the printer – and was considered respectable among magazines of its sort. It was not the equal of its French confrères of course, but was filled with the best expatriate writing. So Dehanty was told. He recognized none of the names when he was shown an issue, and his English was not good enough to know good writing from bad.

It was also said the magazine was a CIA front, which Dehanty discounted. In his experience every American was employed by the CIA and the question of *front* did not come into it.

As for the gun, as it was "in custody" he could not examine it. Dehanty muttered to himself as he walked back toward the Seine through the neighborhood of the Sorbonne that all of these people carried guns. What on earth for? Shooting gangsters, rattlesnakes, and cows?

At an hour well past his usual –

Usual what?

– usual, he returned to the bistro on rue de la Hachette and asked again for Monsieur Caswell Lee. The *comptoire*, a skinny old lady who could have been the mother of the hôtel concierge he had encountered earlier, pointed out a man in a leather jacket eating a *croque monsieur* by the window. It was the man he had seen earlier lying on the bed in the room on the fourth floor.

Monsieur Caswell Lee?

Himself.

Pardon? Oh, I see. Dehanty changed to an English even more impoverished, if that could be believed, than Mr. Lee's French. Dehanty had learned what he knew during the American occupation out of necessity. Many atrocities were necessary then.

What do you want?

I have seen you before, monsieur. The woman who answered the door said you were not there.

Tell me a story, Steve said, abed on a Sunday morning. She was lying half across me but, as it is with old people, ... this ... her ...
out and she rolled off onto her back ... outside when ...
all tangled up there is the problem of ... three and ... so
we lay side by side ... ... naked as two
corpses, and I said.

What sort of story?

A short one I'm getting hungry.

I could bring you a scrambled egg.

And coffee. Yum.

But no, Steve said, before I could ... myself. Story first.

Very well.

... in Paris ...

walk, as ...

a café

... Serl.

... side-

And why shouldn't she? It was no business of yours.

You are the brother of Mademoiselle Constanza, who is arrested yesterday for murdering a café waiter, are you not?

Lee hesitated. Puzzlement flitted through his eyes, perhaps something to do with a mistake in speaking. Then he nodded, acknowledging Dehanty's identification.

She fails to explain herself. Perhaps you can enlighten me?

Not fails, monsieur. Refuses. As I should, since you have not told me anything about yourself.

Ah. My apologies. I am Robert Dehanty, assistant of Monsieur Delarue, the – *comme on dit* – lawyer who is examining her case.

Defending her, I hope.

Eh? Ah yes, *le défence.*

Lee hesitated, clearly uncomprehending.

Perhaps you can tell me something of this, monsieur?

No.

Not? You were there.

No, I can't, and no I won't.

She slapped you on the face just before the – ah, the event. Why was that?

How do you know that? There were only the three of us.

Just as I said, Steve said. Look, can we get on? This law clerk is going to learn nothing from this Caswell Lee. He's wasting our time.

Very well, I agreed. That evening, Dehanty rejoined his – what do they call them?

Boss.

Surely not. Rejoined Delarue to report what little he had learned. The recitation had not got far when there was a rap on the door and a police inspector stepped through.

Entrée, said Delarue belatedly, with some irritation.

Janvier, the inspector said. I've come to tell you concerning Madame Constanza Lee –

Who? Steve said with great annoyance.

Look, I had to come up with a name on the spot.

I represent her, said Monsieur Delarue.

Yes, so she says. That is why I've come to tell you that he has shot a café waiter.

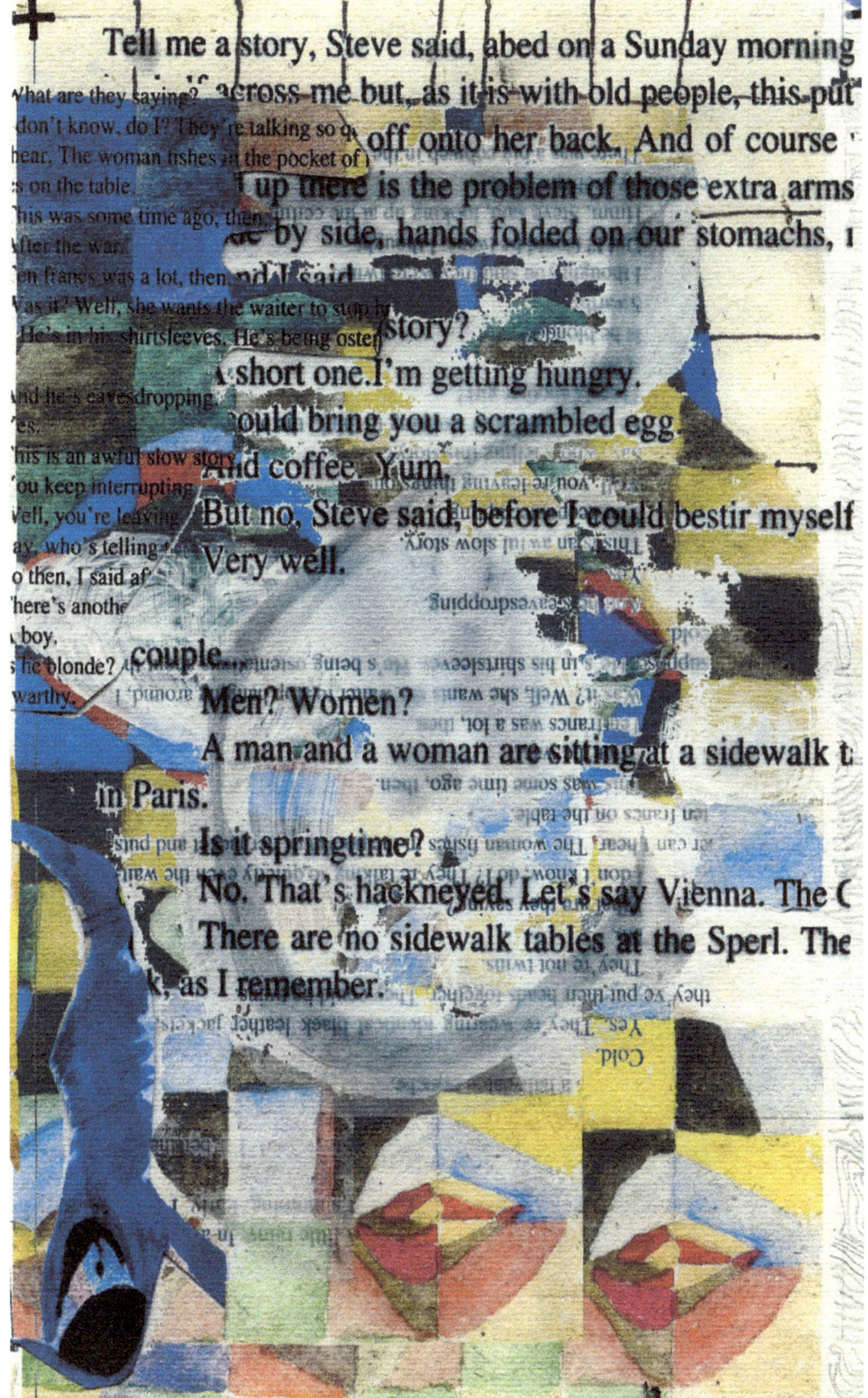

Tell me a story, Steve said, abed on a Sunday morning

off onto her back. And of course

up there is the problem of those extra arms

by side, hands folded on our stomachs,

story?

A short one. I'm getting hungry.

could bring you a scrambled egg.

And coffee. Yum.

But no, Steve said, before I could bestir myself.

Very well.

couple...

Men? Women?

A man and a woman are sitting at a sidewalk t

in Paris.

Is it springtime?

No. That's hackneyed. Let's say Vienna. The (

There are no sidewalk tables at the Sperl. The

k, as I remember.

Yes, We know that, do we not? That is the basis – well, never mind. This Janvier is incredibly stupid, he thought.

No, no, the inspector said. You misunderstand. She has shot him again. A second time.

Delarue and Dehanty were stupefied. At last Delarue managed to croak out a question. Was he not dead?

Oui, oui, certainly dead. She managed to escape from custody somehow, inexplicably recovered her gun, went to the morgue, and shot him. In the head. As before.

Steve barked with laughter. Did you think that up yourself?

Well, who else, I replied shortly, annoyed.

Quite a puzzle. Recondite, I might say. Do you have a suggestion?

I suggest you figure it out yourself, I said sulkily.

THE LAST OF HECUBA

Steve climbed back into bed with her hair wrapped in a towel, looking pleased with herself. I've thought of a story, she said. It came to me in the shower.

Let's hear it, then.

Priam and Hecuba are watching the sack of Troy from a high window in the palace.

What do they want? Hecuba muttered.

Want? Priam replied. Truth, justice, beauty…

We don't have those things. What good does it do to tear up the place looking for them here?

It's because of Hector, I suppose, Priam sighed. He must have given them the idea.

What idea? Hecuba asked, dubious.

Why, that there was something here worth all that cutting and hacking and stomping about. What, Priam pointed out, would they have thought it was he was defending?

Money, Hecuba grumbled. Power, revenge, blood thrills. Such what not.

I would have thought, Priam said, an opportunity for self-actualization.

Hecuba considered. Yes, she said, I suppose they're tired of camping on the beach by now. Singing those drinking songs.

I'll be glad for an end to that, Priam said.

Hecuba looked more closely at the goings on down below. The little Greeks were swarming up the hillside while the bigger men bided their time, waiting to take for themselves anything interesting turned up. She wouldn't have thought you could burn down a stone building but there it was, going on down there.

Don't lean out so far, cautioned Priam. It isn't safe.

Hecuba stepped back. Achilles was one of those waiting for their prizes. Time to come he would claim Polyxena, her daughter.

The thing is, she said, mystifying Priam, Achilles is dead.

So he is, my dear.

So Xena will have to be dead too. Otherwise how…

It's a mad, bloodthirsty business, isn't it?

They're hungry for it, Hecuba said. Dead, every last one of them.

I suppose, Priam agreed, trying to be kind.

What? Suppose? Don't you know?

Let's not start on that, Hecuba. You know – that is, we've never agreed on what it is possible to know.

You could go down and ask them, Priam. There is such a thing as evidence.

What? Down there? Priam was aghast. I suppose, he went on, my empty head might be easier to cut off. Less resistance.

Harder, Hecuba replied harshly. Why do you think it was empty in the first place?

Cassandra came in with half a buttered bagel from breakfast. She wore a white gauzy thing which Priam believed was called a peignoir which it was better not to notice. Matters of this sort probably explained why nobody paid attention to what she said.

You know how this is going to end, don't you? Cassandra said, not quite awake and still irritable.

Oh, yes. Priam took a somewhat macabre pride in this knowledge. We're all going to die, he said. Agamemnon will take you off home where his faithless wife will murder him. You as well, of course. Poison, I believe. Perhaps you could find something else to wear? Less, er, problematic?

Cassandra allowed herself a sour smile. Your attitude is a bit outmoded, Father. We Trojan women are not all complicit in our fates.

That fool Odysseus, Hecuba put in, talks about the wisdom of sucking up to the inevitable. Wear what you want.

I believe I shall go naked, Cassandra said, licking her fingers and glancing toward the window. Terrifying screams could now be heard. After all, she went on, they do. I've always wondered whether the excitement of it all might get in the way of the hacking and chopping.

Mistakes are made, said Priam dryly.

Yes. And you, Mother. What will you wear when you tear the eyes out of that Poly-whosis. I can never remember their names. It's like a Russian novel.

Hmm, was Priam's only remark to this. He was tiring of the morning's talk. I'd better go and get ready, he said.

When Hecuba and her daughter were alone, Hecuba fell into a more somber mood. We will all be raped, of course.

Oh, indeed.

We're not going to have our arms and legs torn off, I hope, like some of those poor wretches. She moved toward the window and then thought better of it. That's a mercy.

Mercy! Cassandra cried angrily. What's that?

Well, dear, Hecuba said, giving her godstruck daughter a hug. When you know everything there's not much room for illusions, I suppose. Perhaps we should go down. People will be stopping by. Nothing has been right since that idiot Paris decided to buy a yacht. You warned him what comes of adventuring.

Cassandra was silent.

I've been putting up tears and purple lamentations since then, Hecuba went on. There are thousands of bottles in the cellar. It's time we cracked a few, before they turn to vinegar.

With that, Hecuba and Cassandra went down amid shouting and the sound of broken glass.

I said: How does this foofaraw about Hecuba and the fall of Troy advance the problem?

You're too impatient, she said testily.

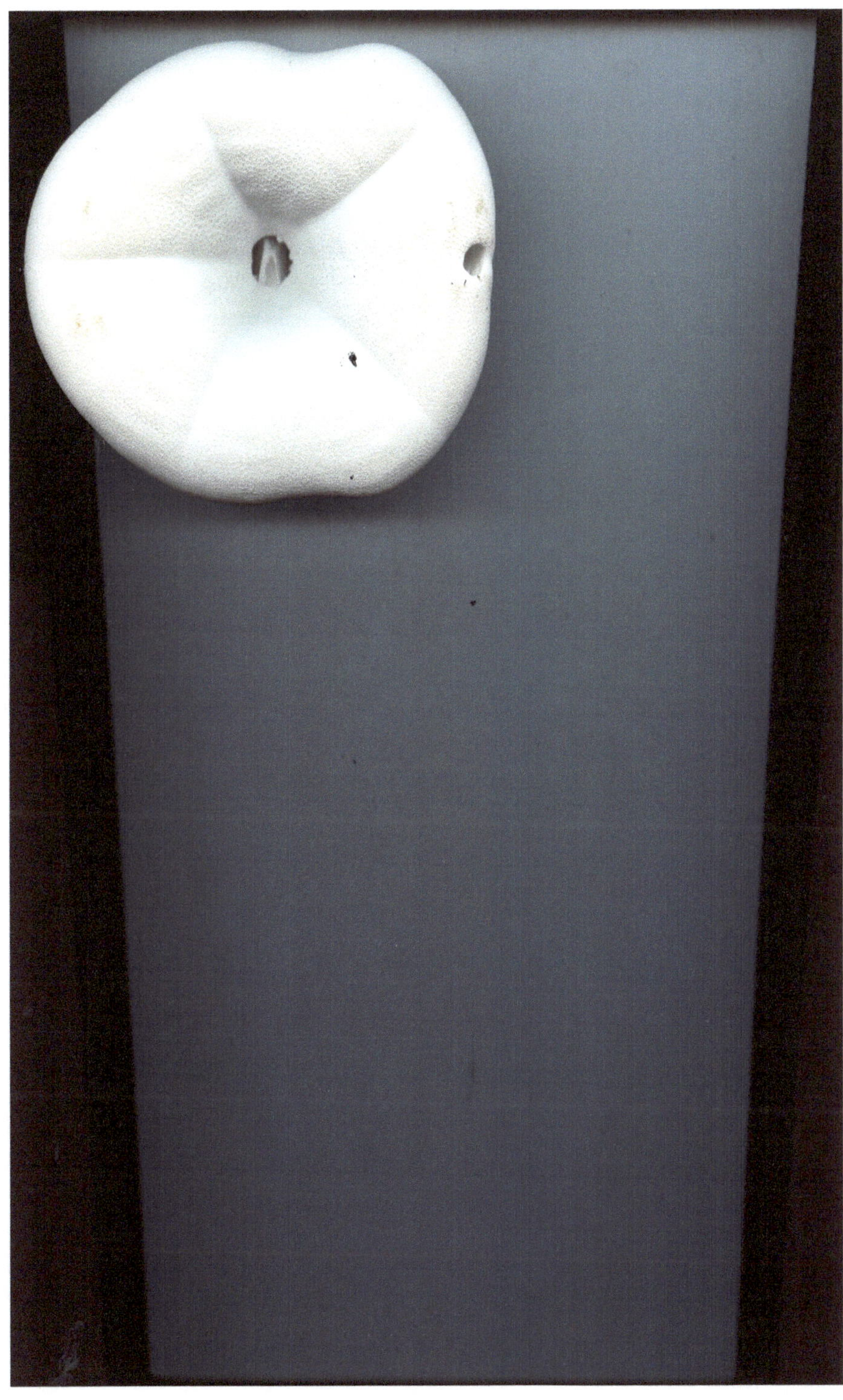

By the next morning the Inspector's news had convinced M. Delarue that he was in over his head, and he instructed Dehanty to engage the services of a private investigator he had used before, a man named Achille. And the day had not advanced beyond the mid-morning coffee before Achille made his appearance, closing the door discreetly, taking no notice when Dehanty burst it open again moments later. Achille calmly took off his hat and wiped the inside band with a checkered cloth, then his forehead. He put the hat tidily on a side table, folded the cloth into a neat square which he put back into his coat pocket, then took off the coat – thickly made out of a soft dark cloth resembling moleskin – and laid it across the back of a nearby chair. On this he sat. From an interior pocket he produced a cigarette case, from which he selected one, lit it, and drew the smoke in deeply.

Bon, he said, the smoke re-emerging in a puff like cotton wool. It is a pleasure to see you again, Monsieur Delarue. How may I be of service?

Delarue gestured with two fingers to his clerk, and Dehanty related what had happened the day before.

Well, Achille said after a pause. That's unusual.

Yes, said Delarue sourly.

Achille's cigarette was finished. Dehanty offered him coffee, which he declined. Uncrossing his legs and straightening the crease of his trousers, he leaned forward, his elbows on his knees. Now let me see, he said. Miss Constanza Lee has apparently murdered –

Apparently, monsieur! She killed him point-blank on a public street.

Yes, it seems so, said Achille with faint amusement. She neither admits no denies the allegation – Achille held up his hand to forestall another objection from Dehanty – and declines to explain herself. You have been engaged, monsieur. Why do you give yourself the trouble of attendance on a magistrate rather than dispose of the matter in the usual way?

The matter is not to my satisfaction, Delarue replied stiffly. I think it ought to be known what the purpose was for this curious behavior, and what justifies her silence. I will not adopt some back-handed defense where a more active one might be mounted. That in not what I am retained to do.

Well, then, said Achille, rising to his feet. I had best go to the morgue and have a look at the damage. You will give me an *entrée,* Monsieur?

Delarue scribbled out instructions on a sheet of letterhead, which Achille took and slipped into yet another of his pockets. Stooping slightly to pass the door, in the hall he straightened and put on his hat. Good day, he said, shrugging onto his coat. You will hear from me after lunch.

Good man, Delarue murmured, and then called out – Dehanty!

Oui, Monsieur. *Votre plaisir?*

See where he goes.

Perfidy, I grumbled. These suspicious lawyers. So – is anything to be gained by trying to decode your allegory, or perhaps roman à clef?

No.

Is there any connection at all?

I doubt it, Steve said. I thought her tone was smug, and said so. My complaint was accepted with a shrug.

As good as his word (Steve went on with the story) Achille re-appeared a few minutes after lunch was finished. After repeating his fastidiousness concerning hat and coat and cigarette, he told them what he had learned.

I begin, he said with some complacency, with the fact that there are two of them.

Dehanty objected to this, as did I. Nonsense. She is far too recognizeable to be mistaken.

Yes, Steve agreed, and Achille averred quietly – one might ask, I think, why she is so noticeable, that one.

Nevertheless, he said more briskly, it is true. There were two. A few simple inquiries were needed to establish this: at what time Madame was served her supper, at what time the gun was recovered from Properties, at what time the morgue was left unguarded when the watchman went out for a smoke. All these things are attested. The two of them made some small errors in timing. It is incontestable.

Recovered from Properties? Delarue inquired.

Yes. The person in question was perfectly correct. She –

the clerk assumed this; indeed, he remarked on it particularly as unusual – presented a signed order counter-signed by the person of Constanza Lee.

What panache! Delarue remarked. He seemed pleased. And who, he went on to ask, gave this order? The Inspector? Dehanty, what is his name?

Janvier.

Oh, yes. Improbable, I believe you said, and with this I agreed. I complained, in fact, quite loudly.

You did not, Steve replied heatedly. It was you who supplied the name.

Did I? Well, let's get on, then. Aside from this business of who was where when, what else does this Achille know?

Suspecting naturally the signature would not be Madame Lee's, Achille said, I took the trouble to obtain her residency permit. Someone else counter-signed that permit. Who, we do not know.

And who authorized it? said Delarue. This Inspector Janvier, you said.

No, Monsieur Delarue, I did not say that.

The Magistrate, then, I suppose.

No.

What? Then who?

The head of the Sûrété.

Ridiculous.

Ridiculous, I said. Why would a person of such a rank interfere is this small matter?

Steve shrugged. It is something to be explained, isn't it. You are impatient. Impatience ruins the fun. The answers have to be saved to the end Then at once, everything is clear. That is how a detective story goes. Unlike life.

She turned her back to me in order to switch on the bedside light. Outside, the weather was overcast and dark. A November rain was predicted.

I'm going to put on a sweater, I said, getting out of bed.

Throw that quilt back on, too, will you?

Now then, I said when I returned to bed.

"Now then" is an odd thing to say, Steve remarked. When you

think about it. One can't say "then now" can one, though it makes sense. It rccapitulates the order of history, whereas "now then" constructs the evidence to form a narrative about the past which fits the circumstances now. As they are now construed. The evidence, you see, exists only in the present. There is no direct experience of the past, which does not exist and must be invented. This is the way of the detective story, isn't it? We are given a narrative, from which we construct a story about the past. The detective deconstructs this. Then now, the keystone is put into place, and *voila!* All is clear.

That's a mixed metaphor,

Oh, lá lá. You are so particular. It goes with your impatience.

Look, Dehanty said. Can we get on? He was stung by the suggestion that he had not been thorough in his research the day before. But Achille pointed no fingers. You have established the players, he said. Now it is my turn to read the lines. But there is one more thing.

Which is?

Monsieur Caswell Lee is not the brother of Madame Constanza. He is her husband.

Dehanty was outraged. Then who, he asked, was the woman who opened the door to me in that disgusting hôtel? It was most certainly not Constanza.

Yes, Achille said quietly. Monsieur Lee, it would seem, is having an *affair*.

The slap, Delarue said with satisfaction. Dehanty, didn't I say?

Dehanty, however, kept his thoughts to himself.

You owe me a long one, Steve said a couple of weeks after the Hecuba story. These Sunday morning stories were beginning to be hard to make up on the fly. Simple enigmas, pseudo-haikus, were no longer good enough. Not stories exactly, which don't hang around waiting to be told, despite what some people think.

Wait a bit, I said to gain time. I want to wash up. I'm all sticky.

That was true in fact. In the shower I thought about growing up, when we had only a tub. Growing up is always a good place to find stories. More like a tar pit than a well, actually, but still. You find the bones there.

I've been showering sitting down for a while now. It facilitates getting to places otherwise a problem like my back or the soles of my feet, but mostly it's the mindwashing fall of water over my head. Somewhat disorienting, this is likely to lead to a mis-step if I'm standing up. So I sit. Like in a tub.

The problem is to get out. I crawl. I towel off sitting down these days, too. The older I get the closer I get to the ground.

Back in bed I met with an offer to get sticky again but I thought it best to embark instead on the real problem. This is itself a big change from the old days.

the old days

I

I said, I'm going to take the sins of my fathers –

You can't do that, Steve said. That's a Tom Waits song. You need permission.

Not. – down to the river and –

You forgot the sins of your mothers.

Will you shut up? This is not a gender parity thing.

The thing is, she said, you don't have any fathers.

That's why we're going down to the river.

Creek, It's a muddy old creek and you're not going to wash anything in that.

OK, I said, exasperated. We'll go somewhere pristine like the headwaters of the Mississippi. Bemidji or thereabouts, I think.

That's too far to carry a load of sins, she said. And there's mosquitoes. The big dive-bomber ones.

When I was nine or ten, I said, we went to stay for a week with an old couple on a lake there. One day we drove from their cabin to –

Itasca. The Mississippi starts there.

Where there was nothing but a little rill and some stones. I didn't understand.

You should have stayed home.

Later we went fishing. I caught a fish, but the man said we had to put it back because it was too little. Later on I found out it was because I didn't have a fishing license. I suppose he thought I would be too stupid to catch anything.

It's always better to stay home, Steve commented.

《 》

In a pique, I went into the kitchen to make coffee. After a while Steve followed in her fuzzy white robe and leaned barefooted against the counter.

Move down, I said. You're in the way.

Is this part of the back-story? she asked, not moving. In the older days we find out that Madame Constanza now shoots waiters

because as a child she was made to go to restaurants where she embarrassed everyone by screaming and the waiters got mad and thwacked her. Is it like that? Like that big dog which attacked you when you were delivering newspapers. Traumatized.

No.

Not a newspaper anyway. It was some sort of dittoed classified advertising, wasn't it? How much did you get paid?

I don't remember. Two dollars, I think. On Wednesday. Or maybe Tuesday.

So is this backstory?

No.

Well, Steve said, this stuff doesn't just come out your ear, you know. There's a reason.

Simenon just wrote them. He locked himself in his room and wrote them in a week. There wasn't any reason.

Pish and tish. There's always a reason. It's a *detective* story.

I don't know, I said. This one's getting kind of silly, don't you think? With quantum murders and allegories about Troy and so forth. It's not going to have that flashbulb clarity at the end.

Who uses flashbulbs anymore?

In 1952 they did. Weegee and, um, and – it's going to be like it always is, a muck.

Noir. Is that coffee done?

Brown. It's American coffee. Everything always ends up all brown. I think we ought to start over.

Nonsense. It's that dog again. Get on with the old days. I want to know who did it.

Well, I said. There's Achille, and he needs to know why anyone would shoot a dead man in the morgue where it's cold and you know for sure he's dead. This waiter –

He needs a name, Steve broke in. Let's call him Almovar.

What? He'll be a laughing stock. It's not even Algerian.

Why does he have to be Algerian?

Because he already is. His name is Ammar.

Close enough.

This Ammar, I said, starting over. What is it about him?

Where did she kill him? Steve asked.

In the café. No, you mean where in his head. Like right here, above the ear.

So then his face isn't messed up. You can still tell it's him. "Hey, Ammar you rat, you were supposed to be tearing up the place, not sitting on your ass reading Franz Fanon."

All right, let's try that out. So Achille

would have noticed this mess already, and since he was looking at those thousands of little reports that come in from the hotels every morning he probably had a look at the arrest report too and found out about the neat little hole just above the ear, here. So now what?

II

My grandfather ran a steam laundry, I began. Let's start with that.

I remember that laundry.

He got the steam free from the village power plant. A sweet deal. The village delivered steam heat to everyone. Out in the country it was different of course. People froze to death out in the country. My mom said she ran the car into a ditch on the way home from school. It was her first time behind the wheel.

You said what car but I forgot.

So do I. A Whippet or something. With a tiller. A Gasowski Banana maybe. Grandfather had to come out with the horses. The horses got lost too.

Horses don't get lost.

Only on television they don't. There had to be a rope from the house to the barn to keep people from wandering off and getting lost.

Country people were found in the spring, you said, two yards from the back of the house.

It was just as bad in the summer. The dust you see. Or don't see I mean. The truth was in the old days you couldn't see anything, ever. My uncle –

Which uncle?

I only had one. The other one died.

On your grandmother's side. It made her bitter, you said. After that she said no to everything.

My grandmother's people said nay. My other people, with the laundry, were from Yorkshire.

Nay, nay is what, Norwegian? What do they say in Yorkshire? Nar nar?

They say no. I've never been to Yorkshire.

Yes you have. When we went to Newcastle that time. For the boat to Stavanger to study the savage Naynays.

You're being racist. Anyway, Newcastle isn't in Yorkshire.

Humpf, Steve said. Your grandfathers weren't foreigners.

As Told To

The one went back to sixteen-something you said. It's the East Indians and the Iranians who are the foreigners now. We'll be racist about them.

I wrote a book about a Pakistani once.

I read that. He wasn't a foreigner either. His people came over during the Partition.

Well Mexicans, then, I said.

Mexicans were here before we were, Steve pointed out. We destroyed the Hidalgo culture. We destroy everything. It makes me sick.

Achille was on his way along a small street on his way to the café where Ammar the waiter was murdered. He was deep in thought, his hands thrust into the pockets of his coat and his bowler hat pulled down low over his eyes.

Since when have men worn bowler hats? Steve asked.

Since 1952, I said. Achille is the last in a long tradition.

You don't have a bowler.

That's out of fashion. I have a ten-gallon hat with a feather –

That's out of fashion, too.

And a leather pork-pie like the Bad Hats wear in movie westerns who smoke these thin black cigarillos –

A *pork-pie* is what Popeye Doyle wore in *The French Connection.* You don't own one.

Yes I do. And three caps and a real Basque beret –

You said "and his bowler hat pulled down low over his eyes."

Yes, I went on imperturbably. Nevertheless, Achille was not unaware of the neighborhood which he was passing through. On his right stood a building of the Sorbonne with its back turned, a four-story pale stone wall with stacked rows of bleared and infrequent windows. A metaphor, he thought acidly but without rancor. Achille had scant respect for the *Grandes Écoles*, though the respected teachers of his boyhood had all been *écoliers.* It was the life of competition and preferment which he found repugnant. Sent hither to some dreary Norman coast, thither to a dull hamlet on the Flanders border, yon to the Vosges or Gascony, all at the behest

of the supposed needs of some stupid ministry. Not married before
forty for want of funds and a settled life and ending no better off
than some miserable tender of the cash-register at the far end of a
zinque.

On the other side of the street lay a small park,
somewhat brown and tattered at this
season, its chairs stacked and its
paths loud with dried leaves,
but still lovely if now elderly
and fond with the memory of
amorous youth. Achille was
subject to

nostalgia, but now
that he was past his
prime
he had discovered
that joy lay in the
ever-accumulating
presence of these
memories
in

his
daily life.

H e
had freed h i m -
self of the intense
agony of loss.

The past does not exist, he had chided himself, except in the mind, and the mind is always present.

That was a good philosophy for a detective, he thought as he stopped to look at the light and shadow of a brilliant crisp day, anticipating his lunch of thick onion soup and a frugal *vin rouge ordinaire*.

Achille was greatly and complicatedly fond o f simplicity and frugality.

Well, he thought, proceeding on his way, let us proceed on the assumption that this Ammar was dangerous to someone. The hypothesis that he was shot the second time to disfigure him and obscure his identity is nonsense. How could Janvier claim to be uninformed on this point if asked? He is either a fool or incompetent. I think neither.

Nor did Achille think that she had shot the waiter in a pique with his intrusive attempts to overhear a private conversation. With Delarue, he too did not believe it was a *crime pasionelle.* There were, in his experience, not so many of these as leafless old people preferred to think.

Dangerous. Personally dangerous? Or because of something he, Ammar, knew? If so, knew about – ?

Achille came upon the café, a triagular space at the acute junction of two streets. The café itself occupied the third side. Achille paused to look about. There was no one outside; the tables had been stripped o f their umbrellas and the chairs taken away. To either side, the mouths of the streets were closed by pinched buildings, so that it was impossible to see around the corner from anywhere on the sidewalk except from where Constanza had been sitting. Achille walked only meter u p one of the streets, leaned against the sun-warmed stone, a n d verified the line of sight for himself.

He entered the café and ordered an espresso from the only person there. Quite frankly, Achille explained that he was looking into the murder of Ammar two days earlier.

You are his replacement?

As Told To

Oui.

You have not worked here before.

Off and on, said the new man, wiping his hands on his apron in a small gesture of anxiety. I did not know Ammar. They call me sometimes, when someone is sick, or has run off to Marseille.

Marseille, Achille repeated, and looked about him. A short bar, a few stools, two round bistro tables. Above the bar a dozen or so wine glasses hung by the feet. Call from where?

Where is your wine cellar? Achille asked.

Here, monsieur. The waiter tapped the floor with his foot, and Achille rose up to look over the counter at a trapdoor with an iron ring inset into the black wood.

May I see?

The waiter shrugged and bent to pull up the door. Below was a very small spiral stair. The cellar was lit by a timer under the edge of the bar. When the buzzing stopped the light went out.

Suppose, said Achille, you had gone down there for a bottle and the door closed and left you in the dark. Suppose there were someone standing on it, talking to a customer.

There is a telephone, monsieur.

Ah. Not an intercom or something of that sort?

No. The owner had it put in.

So it would be possible, if the café were not busy, as now, to slip down there for a moment to make a private call? An assignation, perhaps, for the evening. Some place in Pigalle?

The waiter regarded Achille with a new suspicion. *Oui,* he said guardedly. *C'est possible.*

Je comprende là. Merci.

Achille paid and left the café, hands again in his pockets and unfashionable hat pulled forward across his eyes as befit a man engaged in the getting and deployment of knowledge.

So, he said to himself, a word he used to indicate something established, pronounced *zo.* Assuming that the thing is possible, who would Ammar have called?

A series of inferences was assembling itself in Achille's mind. Madame Constanza and her husband arrive and sit down at an outside table – one in particular. Madame is a striking woman, tall and lean

as a dancer, with flaming red hair exploding from under a black
beret and a flamboyant tattoo on her chest and neck visible at the
opening of her leather coat. Her arrival for some reason alarms
Ammar, who makes unsubtle attempts to find out what
she is saying to her companion. Hearing something,   o r
perhaps significantly nothing, Ammar slips away
to pass the word to a confederate. Returning with
a tray, intending to collect
the couple's saucers, Ma-
dame Constanza stands
    up, knocking over
her chair, and shoots
Ammar dead. Then   s h e
sits down
    again to
await the po-   lice.
    Achille
had seen this
    gun
    in the   In-
                                              spector's
office after   his visit to the
morgue. It   was no lady's

Rocket
Ship

handbag weapon but a bulky American gun of heavy caliber.

Suitable for use, Steve remarked, by a man in a leather hat smoking a black twisted cigarillo.

Exactly, I replied.

And where on earth would a slim woman in close-fitting clothes have carried such a gun?

In a shoulder holster, I said. Here, to one side of the breast, nested in the armpit, concealed by the American leather airman's jacket.

And what on earth for?

How do I know? I repeated, not for the first time since the two of us had begun to build this story. She's an assassin, like that woman in the movie. Catherine Deneuve. In *La Femme Nikita.*

This is not hanging together, Steve said in a tone somewhat more than critical. We are no forarder. There are these Algerians, Ammar and the two others –

What two?

The man on the fourth floor and the second waiter. Now, if true, we are talking about a time when Algerians were learning terrorism in a nasty war of independence and were non grata in France –

Still aren't. Remember that couscous restaurant we ate at? You would have thought we were a pair of David Bowie's Starmen. Certainly not French.

What I mean is, Steve pushed on impatiently, we have Algerians and American spies and assassinations and concealed or obliterated identities and incomprehensible behavior and not a shred of motive. We are emphatically not forarder. Everything we are supposed to know is suppositious –

That's a tautology. Suppositious things —

Get on, damn it, Steve said roughly and unkindly.

The backstory. Grandfathers. Laundries. Square men with square dirty fingernails and square wives with moustaches. Peasants.

III

I remember staying at the Home Farm, I said, one summer. Well it was the Home Farm then, before my cousins all went out and bought more of them and made a Corporation out of themselves. This was before they fixed up the top floor and added a laundry chute. I slept on the rickety porch on a cot. I thought the laundry chute was cool as anything. I would have jumped into it if I'd have fit. I didn't fit anywhere. Even the old cot was too short. There was an orchard then, with plums and chokecherries and wonderful little gnarly apples. I remember Thoreau talking about wild apples.

You don't remember that. What happened to the orchard?

It died. They do that. In the basement there was a generator which they ran to make electricity for the washing machine where the clothes came down the chute and sometimes a cat. The orchard was getting old even then. Probably some uncle's grandfather planted it.

Was the orchard a sin, then?

Get off that. I'm sorry I mentioned it.

Anyway, it would have had to have been planted by Indians if it was that old. Indians don't do sins, I think. East ones maybe. Not West ones.

Jeez. Why did I start this story?

You were playing for time, Steve said.

Well I had to start somewhere, didn't I?

Steve considered this.

No, she said, not just anywhere. These stories are told backwards. They begin with the invocation of the Detective. At this point the crime is done. We know it by hearsay, when the tale is told to the shaman who is going to interpret it. The first direct experience we have is not until the detective's inference chain is grounded, often by a second murder, Sins, you see. Then the whole thing turns into present fact. The beginning of the true history is in the past. If this is a true story it starts in the past.

It's not a true story, I objected. The past is an invention for explaining the present.

As I said, Steve repeated pointedly. Without the crime there is no

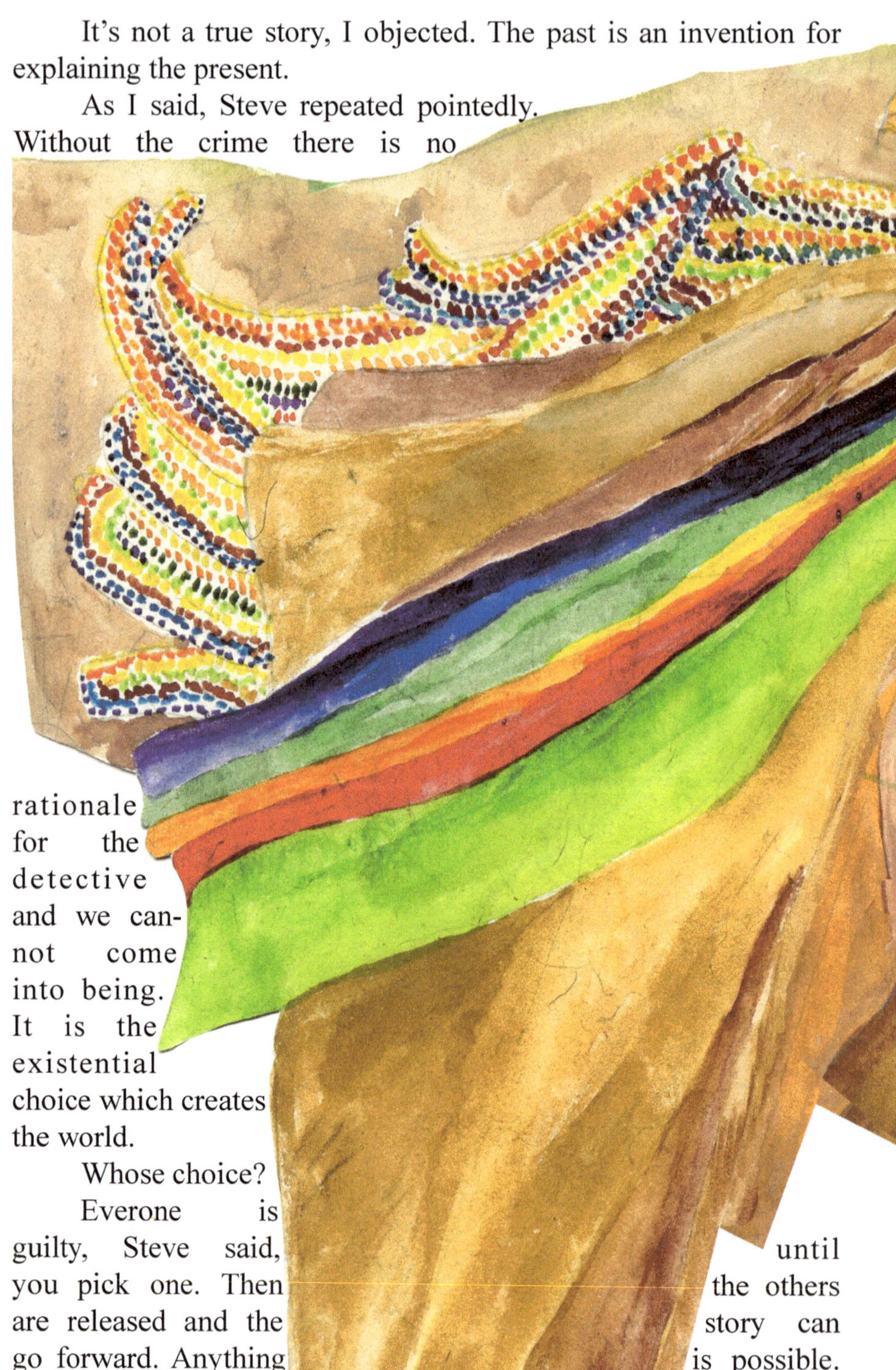

rationale for the detective and we cannot come into being. It is the existential choice which creates the world.

Whose choice?

Everone is guilty, Steve said, you pick one. Then   until the others are released and the   story can go forward. Anything   is possible.

Once you choose, there is only one thing. The rest are red herrings. We tell ourselves these stories because we are desperate for meaning but don't want to give up our comfortable, inauthentic lives. You

can't get away with that.

Nonsense. I can tell this story any w a y   I like.

Yes, until you tell it that way. Then you're screwed.

I said, tentative analysis.

somewhat cautious and in the light of Steve's Two things, I said, are needed to make sense of Achille's inference chain. We need first to know who is to be assassinated and why this particular café was chosen and we need some corroborating fact to ground one end or the other of the chain. That's three things.

So, I said. We have the Algerians and the American CIA

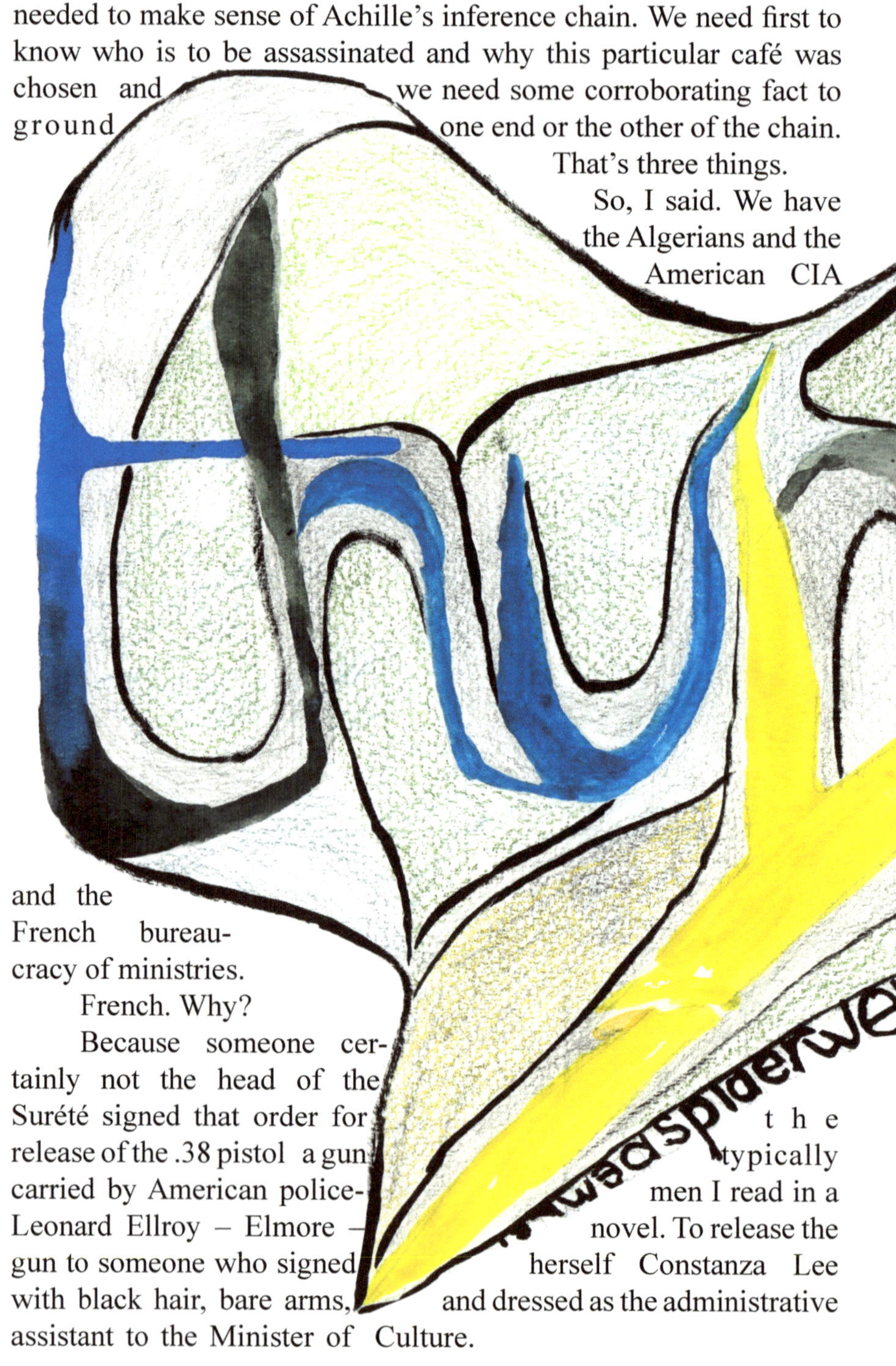

and the French bureau-cracy of ministries.

French. Why?

Because someone cer-tainly not the head of the Surété signed that order for release of the .38 pistol a gun carried by American police-Leonard Ellroy – Elmore – gun to someone who signed with black hair, bare arms, assistant to the Minister of Culture.

the typically men I read in a novel. To release the herself Constanza Lee and dressed as the administrative

Ah. Yes, the French.

There are several lines of inquiry. Who was that woman? Who was the man on the fourth floor?

Peter Lorre.

That was the third floor. And who are these two, Dum and Dee, who are part of the scene at the *Brown Paper Wrapper?*

Who?

That couple, the poet and the painter, t h a t

Dehanty turned up. They've been forgotten, never a good thing when one is looking for suspects. Which line do you think?

Leave aside the ministry. For the moment, opaque. The 'zine, I think.

Good, What are their names, these two?

rock cuts scissors Do we have names? Jules and Jim? Ford **scissors covers paper** and Chrysler?

paper smashes rock Dehanty supplied some names, Steve said. I didn't like them. Too ethnic.

spiderweb catches thunder These are ordinary American men driven out by sexual prejudice and looking to live peaceably among other artists. Names like David and James.

Fine. David is the poet. He's published some things in the

Wrapper of course, and in the other expatriate magazines, and some respected British little magazines, and is beginning to make a serious reputation. He's been to Black Mountain and studied with Charles Olson. Maybe for our purposes we don't need to read any of his stuff.

Why not? said Steve cruelly. Nobody else does, either.

Given that, I refrained from creating any biography for the sculptor James.

If the sculptor had been David, Steve remarked, it would have been thought to be a joke on Michaelangelo.

Look, Steve, can we get forarder here? Someone is always complaining that the other is dragging his feet.

Well what was all that stuff about Achille in the park then? What does that get us?

I won't, I said, be drawn into a defense of art and science swallowed by technology and whether the detection business is coldly rational or warmly intuitive and the cultural significance of the warm-cool narrative and all that because I know that's where that would go because that's where it always goes. Now about the sculptural James and his poetic companion David.

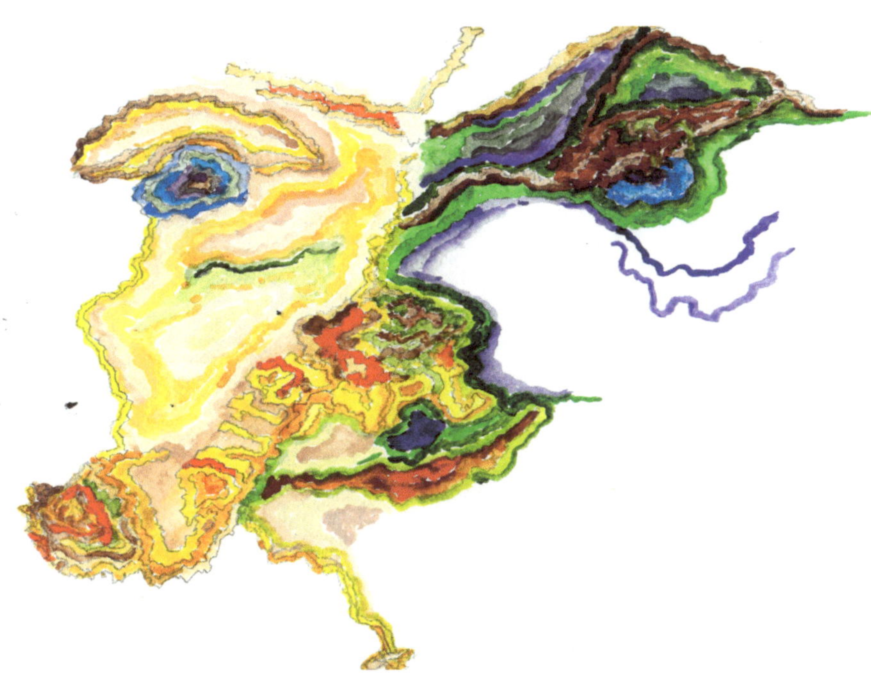

IV

So what about your Father, Steve said. She sounded a little resigned like she hadn't wanted to talk about the Old Days.

He ran off.

No he didn't. That was his first wife. You've got a half-brother in California somewhere.

He's dead.

How do you know? You've never seen him.

Because everybody's dead, that's why.

Because of the sins. Anyway, he didn't run off. He killed himself.

He was murdered, I said.

So you said. Sort of.

He killed himself in an alcoholic depression, or started to, and would have finished the job if he hadn't been drunk. No one called a doctor because he was drunken trash so he died. That's how it was in the Old Days.

Your mother was where?

Yelling for help. I guess they must not have had a phone in the Old Days. The Downstairs People were supposed to call but they didn't.

Nobody had a car?

Not in those days. Before that. The Whippet and the horses that got lost in the blizzard and froze to death.

It was the war. Nobody had a car. Just those little scootery things with lawnmower engines.

They were too poor for a scooter maybe?. It was because of no steam. This was a place without steam where they lived. He was a laundry man, steam or no, because his people had been. The laundry was Downstairs where the People were that wouldn't call anybody.

He got government money didn't he? For the War?

It was from when he fell off the back of a truck when he was drunk. I think it was. Nobody would ever say. In the Army it was OK

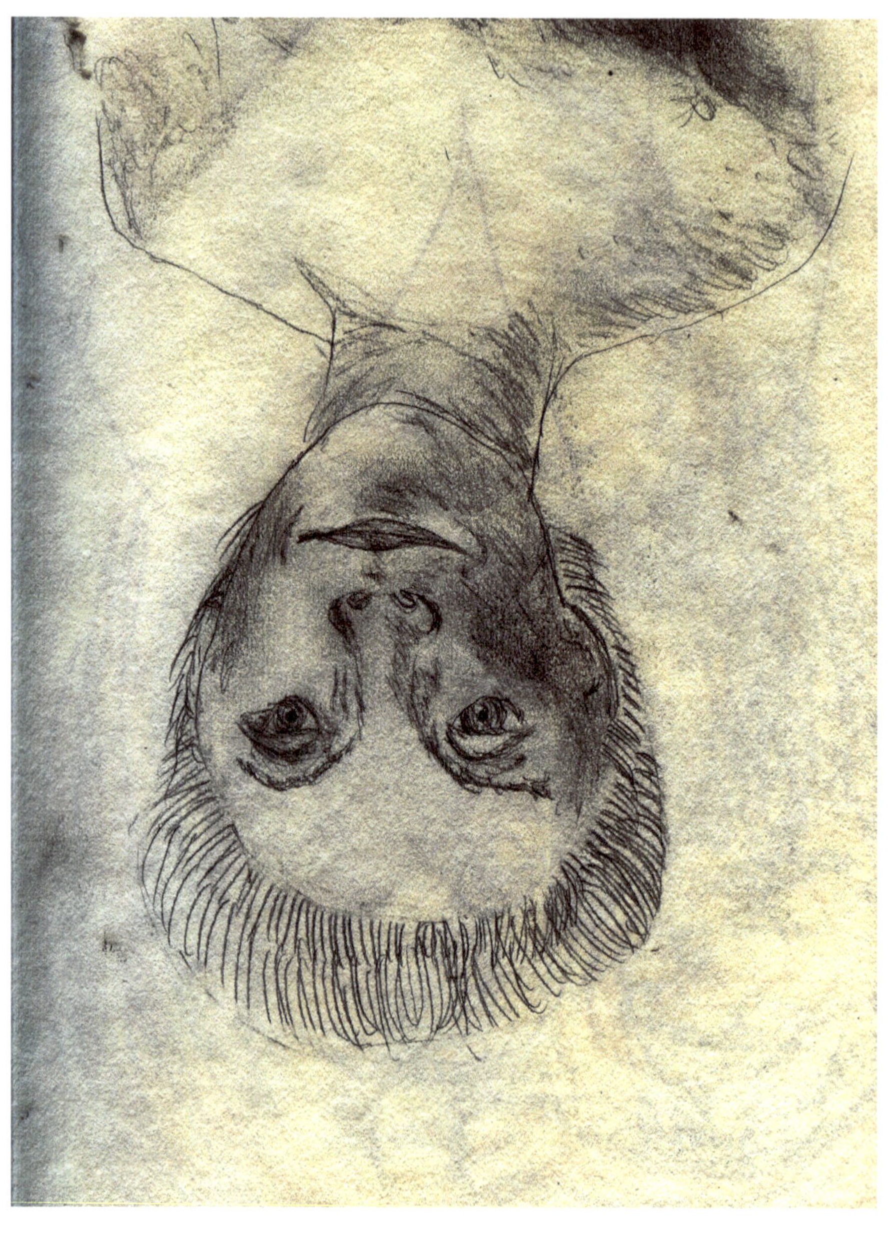

to be drunk so long as they weren't shooting you.

The laundry didn't pay much I suppose. How many shirts could there be in that little town?

No shirtee no tickee, no money.

That was in San Francisco. We got our laundry done next to the Armenian deli.

Yes, with the homemade baklava. Those were the good Old Days.

So what about the Home Farm and the dead orchard and the Whippet in the ditch and the frozen man and the sins? You never said.

I don't remember. That was the Old Days.

Not much of a story, Steve said.

No. It never is.

Who was the second person, the person who shot the waiter in the morgue? If we know that we might know the reason for it. As I see it, the suspects are James, David, Caswell, and Steve.

You jest.

Why not? You're in this up to your neck. You were the one who cast yourself as Hecuba and Constanza as the know-it-all Cassandra and set up Achilles-who-is-dead as this useless P.I. and make jokes about everyone to deflect attention from yourself. You're the one telling this story. You know the answer already.

No, I don't, said Steve, just a little contrite. You're telling it too. Social reality isn't constructed by one person alone. You start a thing but you can't tell where it's going. It's chaotic. Fractal. Quantum. Something.

Well, we're going to look into you along with the others, I said. I was a little angry, and Steve was looking defensive and pained.

Notice, I went on, that I don't include Constanza. I'm taking the description of the person in the morgue at face value.

Why? Steve objected. James is a bald man, short and muscular like a sculptor. If he could make himself into a tall thin *en point* embassy attaché then how hard would it have been for Constanza to put on a wig or something?

Achille went the next day, the third since this open and shut case began, to the offices of the *Brown Paper Wrapper.* Here it was quite as he had expected. He had in fact once wanted to be a poet himself and had spent some time in such places and in the studios of painters and in the dark smoky places where they could all be found when they weren't doing other things. The magazine was located in a couple of rooms at the back of a small building strategically located between two cheap restaurants. On the street side this building had two large dusty display windows behind which were stacked 50-kilo burlap bags of rice, bales of noodles, and other dry staples.

The street door was locked. Achille made his way through a passage and into a small courtyard where he found a second door standing open despite the chill. Three men were there, conferring over some galleys strewn across a high table. Piles of manuscripts covered two desks. Except for a working light on the table the room was dark. In the back shadows Achille could see the door to a second room, closed.

He introduced himself and his business. That he was acting on behalf of Madame Constanza did not produce the welcome he had expected. But then, he had interrupted their business with the galley proofs.

These three men were, excepting Constanza, the whole staff of the *Brown Paper Bag*. He was corrected, with perceptible amusement. *Wrapper*, it was.

Oh yes, my apologies. Achille was abashed. And very slightly warmer. I have two questions, messieurs. I imagine you know the facts. Now: it seems there were two persons concerned in this matter. Madame Constanza and a second woman, presumably a woman, who shot Ammar the second time. My guess is that she works either for your embassy in some capacity, or for one of the French ministries. She is undoubtedly acquainted with Madame Constanza, if only by name or reputation.

Caswell's face was shadowed, but Achille could not see any response to his wife's being said to have a reputation.

Do any of you know who this might be?

No, Caswell said, a little surly.

Look, said David, I'm sorry it's so dark. The switch doesn't work. It never has. Mind the electrical cords.

An English turn of phrase, Achille noted for himself.

You had a second question, the sculptor said, his voice as square and muscular as hs body.

Did I?

In fact, he did, but had decided not to broach it. It was this: if Constanza's behavior in the café was not impulsive but an outgrowth of some plan in the works, as Achille thought it necessary

The forest

to presume, then why had the plan involved this café particularly, and hence Ammar, the regular waiter, particularly?

Instead, he asked whether any of them knew Ammar. None did.

Forgive me, Monsieur Caswell, but he lives on the same floor as your room in the hôtel.

That's not my room. But I know the Algerian you mean. He is not Ammar. As you say, the waiter. I never knew his name.

You have encountered Ammar before?

Certainly not. It was the first time we had been to that café. It is not easy to know the Algerians here. They keep to themselves. A sensible precaution.

Yes. Now to continue: may I ask what you and your wife were talking about?

No. Con shot that waiter for wanting to know that.

She gave you a hard slap. Perhaps her first thought was to shoot *you*, not the waiter.

Caswell's bark had nothing sardonic in it.

Hmm, Achille said to cover the spot.

Will you point out to me where Constanza worked?

We don't have *desks* here. Wherever a space can be found.

Has she left anything here of hers?

That would be a bad idea, James said. The lock doesn't work any better than the light switch.

You could put on something yourself, surely?

What for? We see well enough.

Achille nodded and backed out of the room.

Well, he said to himself out in the courtyard, surveying the windows of the other buildings, I shall see for myself what is in that second room. Tomorrow morning, perhaps. They are not early risers, I suppose.

That didn't accomplish much, Steve said.

It did. I suggested that James is somehow disaffected, and that Caswell continues adamant. Either he cares little for his wife's safety or he knows something which would put her in worse jeopardy. In any case, he won't make something up. It's not in his character.

That, or he's too stupid. In my opinion the sculptor is a thug, and is disqualified by that in addition to his build.

And what, Madame, is *your* alibi? You were there, you can look like anybody you please. That's one of the privileges of indirect third-person narration. And there is a palpable disaffection in you as well.

You were the one, Steve pointed out, who invented this morgue business.

It was a setup.

Several long rancorous moments later, I said: Look, I'm tired of this. We're as predictable as these detectives on television where there is always some status quarrel with his assistant or ill-intentioned interference from her superior.

It's supposed to make them seem more like real people. To make the situation more realistic.

We're supposed to excuse angry snobs just because they're outraged when little girls are raped and dismembered?

Yes, well. Steve paused. But I didn't do it, she said.

I went on with the story. Achille, I said, convinced that the murder in the rue morgue – causing Steve to gag – was not done by anyone in the *Wrapper* coterie, set out to make a systematic search for the *femme* responsible. This James was worrisome, however. He didn't fit in. He played some role in the plot, but what? Achille began by returning to the magazine's office early in the morning. Cigarette smoke was heavy in the air, there was a smell of marijuana and beer, and the galleys had been taken away. The second room he found locked, but the lock was as flimsy as everything else and it was only a matter of pulling the door back on its hinges toward the jamb.

It was a toilet.

That wasn't working either. Achille found a board which could be laid across the sink, and in a supplies closet a neat stack of manila envelopes. Constanza, it seemed, did her accounts *en suite*, sitting here.

Achille remained standing as he worked through the contents of each envelope. They were mostly routine bills for things like paper and postage and printers, laying them in neat piles on the board. There were regular montly receipts for Constanza's $100 – which was a lot of money, Achille reflected, for washing floors or the other sorts of jobs which someone could do who was not French and spoke the language poorly. James only among them was fluent. After leaving the magazine's office Achille had taken the trouble to make the rounds of the important embassies. James was Canadian. A Canuck.

Among the papers neatly filed by date were occasional notes on the letterhead of the Minister for Cultural Affairs responding to requests for support with a trifling few francs, signed Claude Hiebert.

Accordingly, that afternoon Achille went to the Minister's offices and inquired after Monsieur Hiebert.

Madame, certainment.

Is it? I was told – *mais oui, je comprends.*

You have an appointment?

No. You may mention the name Constanza Lee. It's about an expatriate literary magazine which the Minister supports on occasion.

The receptionist picked up the telephone, spoke a few rapid

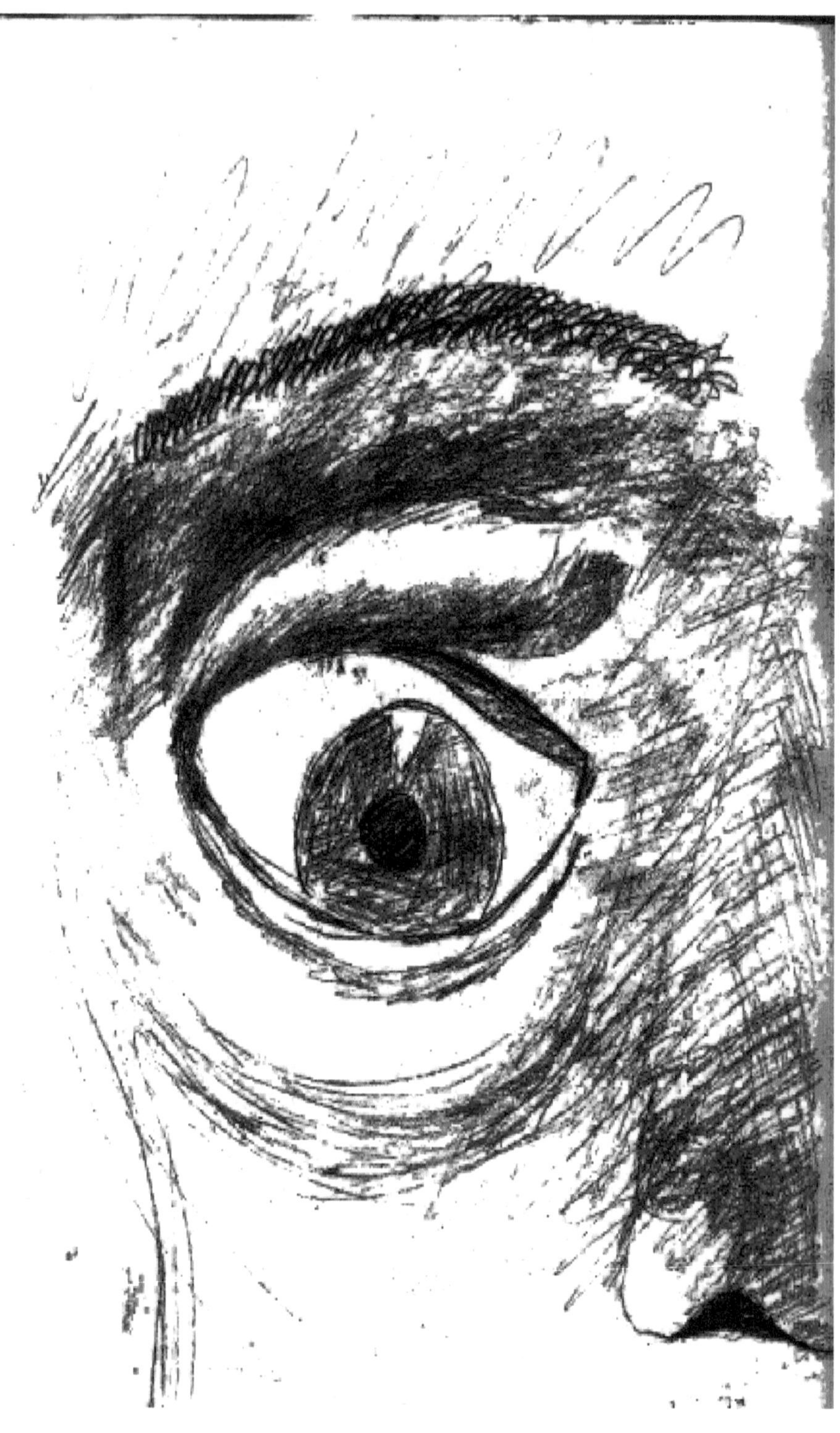

words, and then without replacing the receiver informed Monsieur that Madame Claude was in conference with the Minister.

May I wait? Achille turned his hat between his two hands as if he were measuring string.

There was some squawking on the open telephone line. Hastily, the receptionist cut it off.

Achille reconsidered. Perhaps I won't wait, he said. He had heard distinctly the words "if the Minister" and something else which sounded like *Café Anglais.*

He knew the place. There was a little *croissanterie* across the street with two tables where he could sit and keep an eye on the café's customers. It was not long before a woman dressed in black wearing high heels and a *toque* went in and was served an espresso and a *brioche.* Not long after a man of heavy gravity in a dark gray English suit went in and joined the woman at her table.

Achille had seen enough. Another tour of the embassies revealed that Claude Hiebert was English, deputed by the British Council to liase with the French Office of Cultural Affairs.

Achille grimaced as if he had eaten a moldy grape. *Liase.* An abomination.

He went to sit on the Place de la Concorde, stopping along the way to watch some old men play bocce. The *Place* was a favorite spot of his for rumination. The immensity of it gave his thoughts room to exercise, like

dogs or little boys left off the leash.

In fact, there was one boy in short pants who had escaped his nanny and was zig-zagging about trailing his leash and followed by an equally small woman in a uniform and flat shoes, like a rabbit drawing away the fox from its den.

However, the sun did not stay long and it quickly became cold. Achille drew his coat tight, replaced his hat, and stood up to go. The boy and his *au pair* had given him an idea.

FOUR

RHINOCEROUS

By the way, I said. I don't like that new shampoo you bought. It smells like sweat.

Listen up, Steve said. I'm telling you why I didn't do it. This man and woman — well, boy and girl really — were having tea.

Girl and boy, you mean. Tea.

In that upstairs place in Oxford we used to like. The Nosebag. A winter afternoon. The place was sort of emptied out. They had one of those tables by the window that's hard to get. Mullions and all. The tea was good. Why is it one can't make English tea at home?

Chinese Restaurant Tea, neither.

No. Well, then. It was because they needed to get out. They were tired of chicken tikka and Rennaisance music in the Camera and the train to Paddington. The conversation was desultory. Sloshy winter talk. They were avoiding the Subject, you see, which was that they really didn't want to go Out at all.

This is pretty tired, I said.

Yes, it is, Steve agreed. Who wants to go out in the winter anyway? All that sloshing about. And anyway, people are like that. It's always the same, like dropping stones down wells, you know, or honking in tunnels. You see a hole in the ground you want to jump in. People jump into the Grand Canyon every day. If they didn't haul them away it would be filled up in no time. By the way, you weren't breathing again last night.

Wasn't I? I was having a satori.

You were forgetting to breathe.

"A wind was blowing everything away like rotten clothes clinging to a fence, leaving only the armature."

Like sculptors use to put the clay on.

Exactly. There were these other people, rocks and trees and so forth, that still had their clay on. I felt this great compassion. Love for the things of the world.

You felt sorry for them, you mean.

That's crass. Do you think I'm crass?

Hardly that. Crass has to do with money, doesn't it? Steve said pointedly.

It doesn't. Or only indirectly. This is a long ways from The Nosebag.

Exactly. They were going Out, these two. They were young people in love. They wanted to find their Buddha natures, the Tao. Nothing.

Go back In and fuck, I think.

You're making it hard, Steve said.

I'm sorry, I said, insincerely contrite. I am insincere much of the time. All I want for her is simply to be happy.

You're not happy, Steve said. You're thinking of Her again. You ought not do that, you know.

So why are you telling this story?

Yes, that was a mistake, I think, Steve said. You miss Her, don't you?

I finished my coffee. I don't like tea very much any more, actually, I said.

You've got to stop doing that, she said. It's not good for you.

I suppose.

That wasn't who I meant, Steve said then.

No. Well, we'll get to Her another time.

We need to get out, I said after a while. Where shall we go?

The wineries.

I'm not buying any $150 bottles of wine.

We'll just taste.

They look at you funny.

Let 'em, she said.

Achille was beginning to bring together the strands of the case. The Minister of Culture, he discovered, was said to be planning a compromise concerning some issue in the Algerian war of independence which had quite angered many. There was, in fact, some loose talk about assassination, but where the Algerians were concerned one heard a lot of this sort of thing, and little credence was given it. Achille, leaving the office of one of his many confidantes among the clerks and *functionnaires* of diplomatic Paris – these were the people on whom his success rested – Achille remarked sardonically that it was one of the wonders of France that a culture minister could make anyone at all angry, except for writers, of course.

France has as many of those as cooks, replied this particular informant, who had finished jogging some papers into a neat pile and was putting on his hat, a well-brushed bowler, in preparation for going out. Achille stood in the open doorway, his hand on the knob, paying no attention to the whisking motions of his friend's half-gloved hand, urging Achille out so that they not be seen too much together. *Quelle triste,* Achille had reflected more than once, when so many of one's relations are of this sort.

That's a horrible noir cliché, I said.

Of course it is. How do things get to be clichés in the first place, but because so many people have noticed? It is also widely known that 47 is a prime number –

About as widely known as the fact that all cultural attachés are spies, I interrupted, but with a more conciliatory sharpness. That's a cliché too.

She agreed. But, she pointed out, the spy story is only a noir tale with the moral center hollowed out. Achille is quite right: love is *triste,* whereas intrigue is merely amusing.

There was a reflective pause in our conversation.

You didn't mind too much, Steve said quietly, that I stopped you buying that wine yesterday?

No.

Cheap wine is like a cliché, isn't it? No one wants to admit that it can be quite good. This story seems to have drifted a little ways from the its conventions. I hope it's not turning into a spy thriller.

No more than that one about Cadogan West and the plans for the Bruce Partington submarine.

Such names. *Cadogan.* Who these days would name a submarine Bruce?

What about the *Nautilus*? And the *Enterprise*?

Yes, Steve said. But in this case, I think, the Ministry of Culture has to do with something uglier than that sort of colonialism.

In the office of the friend who wished to remain anonymous, Achille reflected that it was time he brought Monsieur Delarue up to date. A short brisk walk took him there, but Delarue had gone out, leaving his clerk Dehanty to his own business. *Ah, bon jour, Achille!* Dehanty seemed quite delighted by this particular interruption. He, too, jogged his papers into a neat pile and pushed them aside.

Thé, mon ami?

Tea! You have become English?

Certainly, Achille, since you asked me to learn something of this Claude Hiebert.

Ah, yes. And what have you found?

Nothing! said Dehanty triumphantly.

This is significant.

Of course, Dehanty went on with a cluck of disapproval, all sorts of people can be English. Kenyans, Andaman Islanders –

Achille occupied himself with pulling off his gloves, which he laid with some emphasis on Dehanty's desk. This little pantomime had the desired effect.

Some of these expatriate literary people have developed connections with Tunisia, Dehanty said, but not Algeria so far as I know. And of course Madame Claude affects a professional indifference. These people's antecedents are all obscure. Now if they were French –

But they are not, Achille said hastily. And how comes it that a close advisor to the Minister of Culture is an English woman? Yes, yes, she is detailed from the British Council, but *détaillleurs* do not in my experience conduct their affairs in cafés, of which there are many in Paris. Enough to meet in a different café every day of the year, I imagine, though it has been only two weeks. If it is an affair of that sort it is a very clumsy one. And if not, I find it incredible that a Minister should confide matters of policy to the advice of an insignificant, English, woman.

I am reminded, Dehanty mused, of Madame Constanza and her, ah, husband. A similarly opaque relationship.

You do not believe they are married?

No, Achille. Married people do not slap.

Au contraire, Achille began with amusement, thinking to annoy Dehanty just a little over his meager experience, but stopped suddenly.

Sacré bleu! You are right!

Excuse me, my friend, Achille said hastily, and rushed out leaving one glove on Dehanty's desk.

That's enough of that, Auberta said.

THE NAME OF GOD

We were talking of names, I said.

We weren't, Steve insisted.

I continued on. Speaking of names, you used to be someone else.

That was when I was in pigtails.

But everyone called you Steve, even the teachers. Who were you before?

Why didn't you ask me, then?

Squeamish, I suppose. It's like not looking at naked people. Personal. It was a long time before I discovered… well, never mind.

Anyway, she said, it's a secret. Maybe if you'd asked me the first time we went out, but all you wanted was to feel my twat.

Yes, I'm embarrassed about that.

If you'd have listened you could have had me the second time.

Listened to what?

A story, of course. But it's secret.

What good is it then if it's a secret.

It wasn't then. It is now.

I suppose you aren't going to be naked any more, either, I said regretfully.

Probably not.

And just when I'd learned it wasn't a secret.

What wasn't? Isn't, rather.

You… well, never mind.

Some people on the bus who were listening stopped. It was Wednesday morning which is free day at the museum and we were taking the metro in except first you have to take the bus, and the bus came while we were talking so we went on talking. The bus was full of office workers and students. The workers had used so much perfume and aftershave it made my nose itch. The students smelled of pizza and sex and old beer. It was already a hot day which made everything worse. Steve smelled like always, green tea and bagels and some other things, except that she didn't because of the workers and students. Bagels made me think of a breakfast counter in Brooklyn where we ate one time because we were going to the museum and a theater and they had an orange juice maker. You dumped the oranges in the top and orange juice came out of a spigot at the bottom. We tried to figure out where the used-up oranges went but it was no use.

Secrets, I said after pondering the matter, don't seem to be something one can do anything about. They're like the wind or the ocean that way.

I get tired of the wind. It was always windy there. Forty miles an hour day after day, first one way and then the other. Very tiresome.

Over the years you've kept a lot of secrets from me, I imagine.

Only the things you didn't hear because you weren't listening. You're like that crazy woman we saw in Boston.

The Commons.

Yes. Muttering spells, and then stopping to wave her arms and shout Get away! Get away!

It was the flies, I suppose.

There you are. See what I mean?

No.

They could have been demons. She said they were.

There aren't any demons, I said firmly. They're stories.

Steve snorted derisively. What about? If there are to be no demons we should stop telling stories.

I don't believe that's possible. It's one of the first things we did with language. Campfires, how we killed the mammoth.

Oh of course, Steve said, disgusted. Mayhem and sex are all we talk about.

Stories are like that. They don't go away.

You had a good one about that girl you thought about all these years. She was a demon, wasn't she? Not Her, though. I'm still waiting for a story about Her. I don't even know her name. It's like the Hebrew God's name. It's a secret.

It's not, you just can't say it. This is our stop.

We got off and stood on the platform with the workers and students under one of those ramadas. This one had bronze grapes and Mayan sundials on it and a lifesize bronze man with a

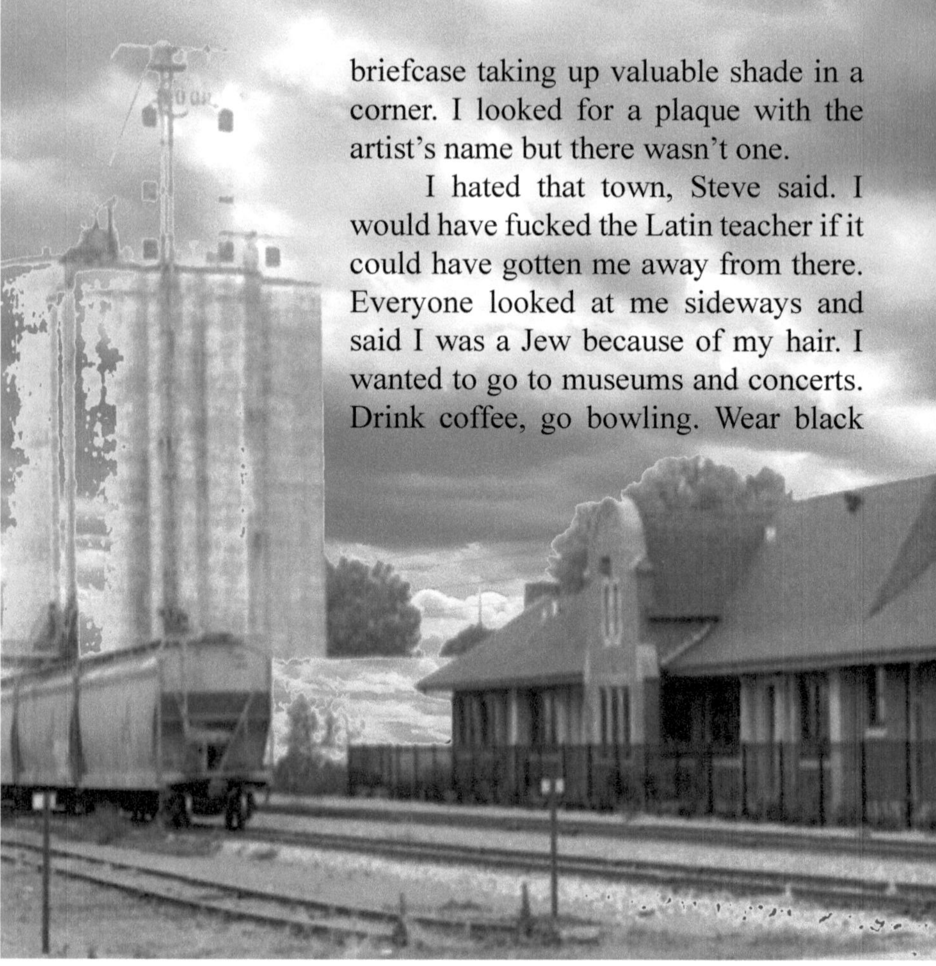

briefcase taking up valuable shade in a corner. I looked for a plaque with the artist's name but there wasn't one.

I hated that town, Steve said. I would have fucked the Latin teacher if it could have gotten me away from there. Everyone looked at me sideways and said I was a Jew because of my hair. I wanted to go to museums and concerts. Drink coffee, go bowling. Wear black leotards and sandals and grow my hair long. It gave me stomach cramps, all that wanting.

You did have long hair.

How would you know? You never saw it. It was black and coarse and I spent hours fighting with it and if I could have just let it loose I would have had some kind of nimbus. Like a saint. I guess there are no Jewish saints, are there.

You aren't Jewish. You're an atheist.

Maybe. You can be both, you know. The other girls were so white they were transparent. You'd be wasting your time trying to feel their twats. You wouldn't have known where to put your hand.

You're bitter.

You wouldn't know. I got over it.

I'm sorry.

.   Steve arched one eyebrow and looked at me doubtfully sideways.

The metro train showed up, sliding electrically to a stop where we stood exactly halfway between two doors. Steve started one way and I went the other except that she grabbed my elbow and put an end to this inevitable minor crisis. All of the students with bicycles crowded on the other way. The doors twitched impatiently.

So why did you go out with me the second time, then? I said when we had got on. We were both hanging from the same strap in the midst of the bicycles. Nobody was listening now because they all had wires in their ears and were talking to somebody else who wasn't listening either, probably.

Maybe I wanted you to feel my twat, she said. Maybe you would take me away from there. But you didn't. I was bitter about that. When you stopped me on the street in San Francisco I should have maced you.

I remember that. You were working in an office somwhere. A bank. You had a valise.

And you were wearing sandals and orange pants.

What was in the valise?

Nothing, Steve said, bitterly.

We got off at the museum. The bicycles stayed on. Since it was too early we went across to a coffee shop for tea and croissants.

This is a story, isn't it? I ventured after a hesitant silence.

Everything is a story, you said, she said sinisterly. Did you remember the tickets?

Tickets? It's free day. And yes, I said. And really your parents were nice people and you didn't have a little brother or pigtails. Your hair was soft and really short.

No it wasn't.

Steve, I remember. You had a butch cut.

It was a page boy. If you'd been listening you'd have known that.

Flowering of a dead sea

Well if I wasn't listening why did you go out with me?

It's a secret, Steve said.

Later, Steve relented. I'm going to tell you how it's going to be, she began.

You can't do that, I objected. That's by Buddy Holly. I used to go ice skating to that. There was a public rink. They flooded a park and hauled in a little hut with a stove to change into your skates and they played that song on the loudspeakers.

That was before me, Steve said. Before I started going to school in town.

Yes. I was thirteen.

That dates you.

You, too. I was just beginning to think about girls. I would skate all around, go round and round wishing I had a girl to skate with. I wore this horrible green coat and all the best girls wore tights and jackets and hats – not those stupid things with the ear flaps like dimestore Russians in spy movies. I was miserable, and they were always playing that song.

Was that our song, then?

No.

All those songs are about getting laid. Well they would be, they're sold to little boys. That was what was so revolutionary about Heroes and Villains, that Beach Boys song.

What was?

Well, Steve explained, it was a grown-up story about falling in love – I mean real love, with sacrifices, people with limitations – and it doesn't go right, but you learn to accept it.

The Dead covered that song, I said. The Buddy Holly, I mean.

"I'm gonna tell you how it's gonna be. You're gonna give your love to me." That's rape, that's what.

We weren't into deconstruction then, I said. I'd rather go off skating alone, anyway. I'd go for miles down the creek, all the way to the river. It wasn't a good idea to skate on the river – the ice might be soft. On the creek the ice was crystalline in the pools. It was so beautiful you almost wanted to walk around it. The slough grass was frozen all tousled like bed hair dusted with dry snow. I found a six-pack under a bridge once.

I suppose you got drunk.

I took it home and put a piece of hamburger in it.

What on earth for?

Because I'd been told that alcohol would rot your guts. Another grown-up lie. The creek went around by your house, but you weren't there. I used to ride my bicycle past all the girls' houses hoping they would come out and say hello but they never did. Were you going to finish this story?

Yes, Steve said. I am. Achille rushed out of the lawyer's office without his hat and only one glove. It was fastest to run all the way, which he did, bursting into the Minister's offices past outraged receptionists and secretaries and breaking the glass in the door in the violence of his entry.

He found three people frozen into a tableau by his explosive entrance. The Minister had just risen to his feet behind his desk. Madame Claude had been standing in front of the desk and now had backed up onto it, half-turned with her hand behind her on the blotter. Facing them, with a gun, was Inspector Janvier.

In the momentary shock of their surprise Achille showed some energy which those who did not know his war experience might not have expected. With a quick blow he knocked the gun to the floor, breaking Janvier's wrist. Then he knocked the man himself down, pressed a knee into the small of his back, and said calmly to the Minister:

You will call for some assistance, Jean-Luc?

Later that afternoon they were all gathered in the lawyer Delarue's office. Janvier had been taken away. Caswell Lee had been found – Claude had escaped the fracas in the Minister's office and turned up at the lawyer's with him two hours later.

Ah, madame, said Achille with a smile. I see you have been to Auteuil.

Claude's eyes widened a tiny bit.

Dehanty was aggrieved. Why was I sent to that hôtel for him?

It was where we made our plans, Caswell admitted. Claude would meet us there. Ammar — Ahmed thought you were from the Minister's office, come to collect her. It was insecure, but had happened before.

Delarue interrupted. Who is Ahmed?

And Dehanty protested. The woman who lived there was Madame Constanza. It was she whom I saw in your bed.

The other waiter, Achille said, with a glance at Claude. On the fourth floot.

Caswell went on complacently. That is what people thought, he said. What we want them to think.

They had all been too engrossed to notice the quiet entrance of Constanza herself. Now she seemed to appear out of nowhere, from a cloud of smoke (of which the room was indeed full), all flamboyant hair and clothes but with her tattoo thankfully covered.

Behold! Crowed Achille at this coup de théatre, which was more than he could have wished. Madame Claude and Madame Constanza: sisters.

Merde, cried Constanza, falling on her. So you're all right.

Twins, in fact, said Claude quietly. And then to Constanza: I missed you at home, or you would have known.

Oui, monsieur, she said, turning to Achille. Auteuil.

Behold! Crowed Achille at this coup de théatre, which was more than he could have wished. Madame Claude and Madame Constanza: sisters.

Twins, in fact, said Claude quietly.

Merde, cried Constanza, falling on her. You're all right.

Now that we are all here, Achille said, I shall explain. But of course, it is those hired for your defense who do not know the truth, he continued with a barb. Nevertheless, there might be some small interest in how I have unraveled this matter. At least, I may hope so. Perhaps some girl will come out to say hello after all, eh?

You have averted a great harm, Monsieur Achille, Caswell Lee said firmly. We do wish it.

Very well. Please dispose yourselves. Perhaps Monsieur Delarue will make some coffee?

I will call for some, Delarue said, and did so.

Delivering the Maltese falcon through the slough to the railhead

Now that we are all here, Achille said, I shall explain. But of course, it is only those hired for your defense who do not yet know the truth, he continued with a barb. Nevertheless, there might be some small interest in how I have unraveled this matter. At least, I may hope so.

You have averted a great harm, Monsieur Achille, Caswell Lee said firmly. We do wish it.

Very well. Please dispose yourselves. Perhaps Monsieur Delarue will make some coffee?

I will call for some, Delarue said, and did so.

It was Monsieur Robert, Achille said, indicating Dehanty, who revealed to me the truth when he said that married people do not slap each other. Be that as it may – and here Achille made a small bow to the blushing Dehanty – his remark made me realize that we had misapprehended the relations among you three, and that this would put a new face on the plans I had uncovered to assassinate the Minister.

Here Achille made another small bow, which the Minister returned.

Madame Constanza's partisanship on behalf of Algerian independence is well known, Achille went on. How could it not be? She is instantly recognizeable everywhere. She is one of those Americans out of the Wild West which we French are so fascinated with. She plays the part a little, I believe, for in fact her views are more peacable. Like her more demure sister, she would rather her cause could be pursued by compromise of the sort which the Minister has proposed. Alas, I fear that is not to be. I had discovered that the Minister — no, no, I must not go on with these foolish formalities — I had discovered that Jean-Luc had for several weeks been negotiating secretly with the Algerian separatists in a series of meetings arranged by Claude Hiebert in small, out of the way cafés. There was a series of go-betweens, of whom Ammar was one. By the way, your friend made a foolish attempt to foist off Ammar as the regular waiter when the truth was the reverse, a lie so easily exposed.

Yes, Claude said. He was afraid, naturally. Ahmed was.

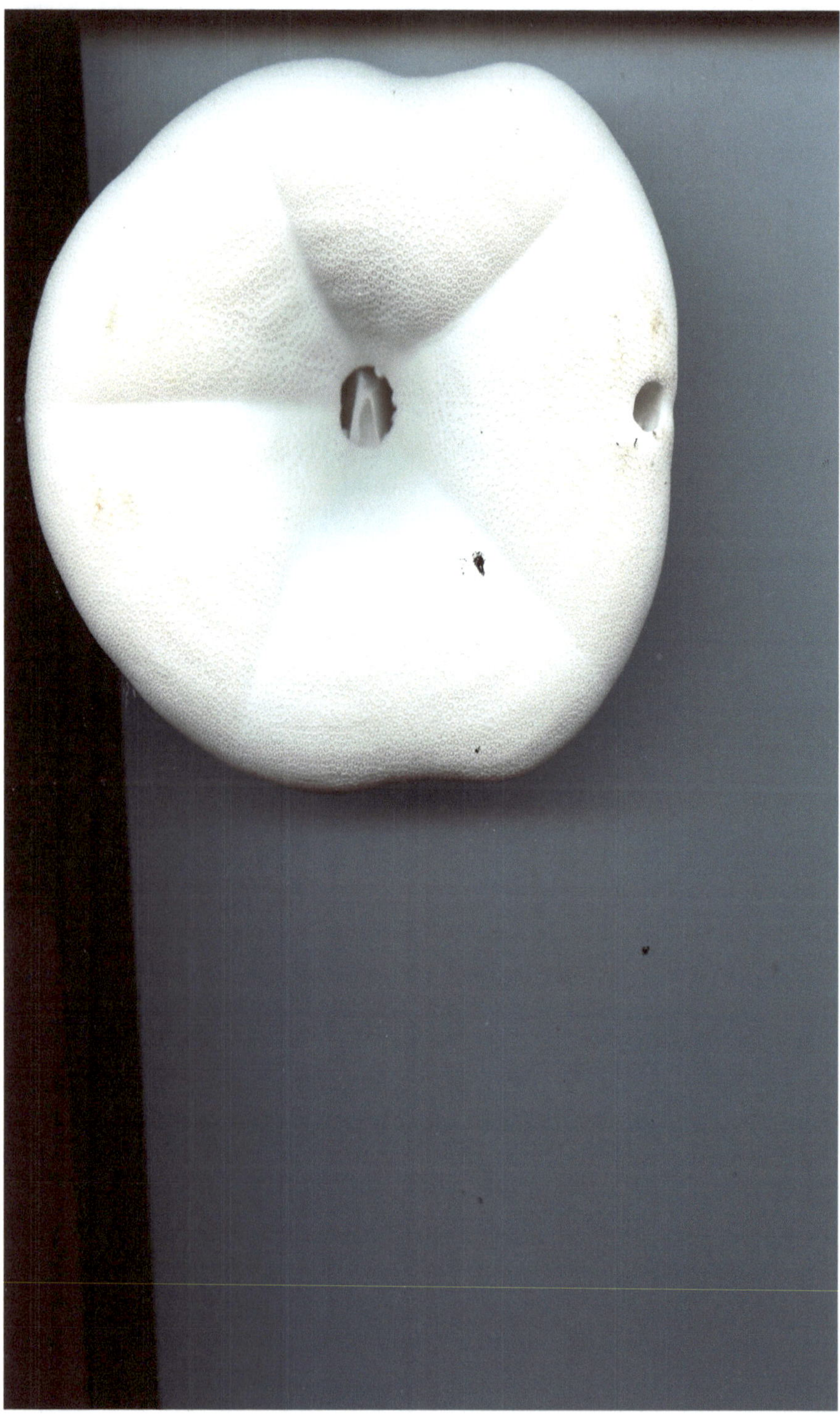

Naturally. Now the unfortunate day. You, Claude, had arranged with Ammar that day's meeting, but at the last minute received intelligence that you were betrayed, the meeting was known, and that the Minister was to be killed . You were not in time to inform Ammar, but were able to find your remarkable sister, who went to the café in your stead. You youself must remain hidden.

Now imagine poor Ammar's consternation. The Minister is not there, his friend Madame Claude is not there, there is only this separatist firebrand, and it is he himself, Ammar thinks, who has been betrayed. He is mortally anxious to know what to do. He goes to make a telephone call. He tries to overhear what you are saying. You are having an argument.

Cas was accusing me of having an affair with David, Constanza said. It was something James had said out of jealousy. I was quite angry with Cas for being so foolish, and at such a time.

You slapped him, Achillle went on. It was, in a way, Monsieur Delarue, a lover's quarrel, eh? Now then. Ammar's behavior had caused suspicion to fall on him. It is the way, is it not. We have a way of creating what we most fear. But you did not shoot him.

No, Constanza said. I didn't.

When I went to the café I could see at once that the assassin had chosen well. It would be possible to make the shot from a hidden position behind the corner of either of the two buildings forming the small triangular forecourt of the café.

I suppose, Delarue said as he was distributing the coffee, that Ammar had attracted the ire of the separatists as much as the Minister had.

Perhaps. But Caswell, you knew at once that the shot you heard was not from Constanza's ostentatiously heavy pistol, which by the way you should never have been allowed to carry. Our government, *Monsieur le Ministre,* is far too lax. It is nearly eight years now since the Liberation.

Achille, *mon ami,* we collect the taxes, we encourage writers, and we see to it that a loaf of bread is genuine, baked on the spot. We can't do everything.

Yes, you have your priorities. Fortunately the French, too, are interested in bread and writers, though perhaps not so much in taxes. Now Constanza: you are in an awkward position. You have apparently shot the waiter. To run will make you a fugitive and defenseless, to deny the obvious will seem lunatic. Moreover, any unwise word will jeopardize your sister Claude, who must guard her cover for the Minister's sake as well as her own. Everyone must be mum. *C'est le mot,* mum? Madame Constanza is arrested, her gun is confiscated, and you, Caswell, seek out Monsieur Delarue for help, who in due course asks for mine. Bon.

Now this Inspector Janvier arrives with the surprising news that Constanza, while in custody, has somehow contrived to recover her gun, which is as distinctive as she is, go with it to the morgue, and shoot her victim a second time. This is so crazy as to be unbelievable.

Achille, said Delarue impatiently. *Who shot the waiter?*

Janvier, monsieur. He had gone there to kill Jean-Luc. It was Ammar who betrayed you, Achille said, turning to the three conspirators. Janvier thought Ammar was about to give the game away. When he saw you standing there with your own gun a new possibiity arose. You would hold the sac. But Janvier's gun was a small one. A *French* gun. What ought to have been obvious was that, in order to make it appear that Constanza had shot Ammar it was necessary that it be so.

Yes, said Caswell with a laugh. That is the way of things, Achille, as you said.

Why did you not protest this nonsense?

Who to? I did not know myself who shot Ammar, so how could I guess who shot him again?

Yes, Achille went on. Now if I had seen, as I should have, that Janvier had shot the dead man, which he could so easily do, then it would be clear that he had shot the living one as well. You see the absurd story it was now necessary to tell. Once my attention was no longer fixed on *le sac brun* I thought: if Janvier did not see at once that Ammar was not shot with a .38 then he is an incompetent imbecile. Since he must have known it, why did he not say so? Instead, he sends us off to Constantinople where we would have gone in any case, buying the tickets and waving bon voyage.

You wrongly assumed, I suppose, interjected Jean-Luc Morny, that the person who shot Ammar was a separatist who found compromise repugnant, and so overlooked the policeman.

Yes. And such was actually the case, except that rather than seeking Algerian independence the murderer of Ammar and your potential assassin wanted to destroy the separatists by inflaming the public with an outrage. You know, of course, Jean-Luc, that such a group exists and that Janvier is a member of it. These people are deluded, unfortunately, as to the French public's tolerance for

outrages where the Algerians are concerned. They have come to expect it. Such are the wages of terrorism.

Well, Achille went on, with Janvier's help or no I was soon almost fatally off in the wrong direction pursuing an imaginary hare through the bushes. If such is the case, I say to myself, then this or that person will have done what or whatnot, but from that person's view the situation would appear to be such and so, leading them to concoct this explanation to cover up that which they believed to be so, which was not so. One could be snagged in these bushes a long time, and meanwhile a government minister is assassinated, a war turns increasingly ugly, and an innocent woman arrested for a crime of passion is executed for the very act of terrorism which had been expected of her.

Madame Constanza, Monsieur Dehanty said quietly, but somehow in a voice which commanded the room instantly, why do you live in this way, so conspicuous as to be a danger to yourself and to draw down opprobrium and contempt?

Everyone was taken aback, perhaps not the least Robert Dehanty himself. He had drawn a clear line between two ways of life, but in defending his own inconspicuous way he neither claimed its superiority nor withdrew his sympathy for the other. And it was this sympathy which surprised everyone.

As Told To

Flowering of a dead sea

Thus challenged, Constanza and her sister drew together. Side by side it was easy to see they were twins, together the embodiment of what Dehanty had said. But *le feu* Constanza had the true redhead's translucent skin, while the shadowy black-haired Claude was merely pale.

Well you see, said Madame Claude, it is so easy for each of us to become the other. When you are Constanza, no one thinks it necessary to find the tattoo.

Claude opened her blouse at the neck to reveal a bit of a large and colorful tattoo which seemed to be that of a bird.

So then, Achille said impishly. It was not you, Claude, who were seen leaving the morgue that evening, but your newly-demure sister, who had just shot a dead man with a .38 pistol, a comedy which no one would believe. A more plausible truth would be the one which I have explained. Ahmed could be passed off as Ammar, who is still alive and now wiith a free hand.

The room burst into laughter, Steve said, but I noticed that Caswell and Constanza exchanged a brief look in which I could read the complicity of a brother and sister who had been conspiring together since childhood in such games.

So now it starts all over again, I said ruefully.
Stories do that.

SIX

About Lettuce

I'll not ask you for a story, Steve said some weeks later, after an abashed respite. That slipped a bit out of hand, I think.

Nevertheless, I replied –

Oh dear, it was now her turn to say, quietly to herself.

I shall tell you one. But on a quite different subject, I assure you. I'm to blame for mentioning sins in the first case.

Yes, she agreed. I've never quite understood what those are. Little nuggets of something that gets into things, like crumbs into your teeth. It's the way people talk, you know, about chocolate and perfume and so forth. I can't quite think that can have been the original intent, no matter how daft.

At this time I had been in the mountains for a month. Steve had stayed behind, having found a co-op studio in which to work and reluctant to pass up the opportunity. She had been able to make a few pots, of which there was now a small show on the dining room table among the tea things. I had been turning several of these over in my hands while Steve poured. Taking tea rather than coffee at these times had come to seem a good idea.

Pours well, I observed of the new pot. Good balance? Handle's a bit small for me.

You don't drink tea.

I've changed my mind. You must remember that museum in Tokyo. One would have liked to feel – that is, to handle them. What they're like in the hand.

Hmm. Famous old tea bowls with individual names, national treasures, I can't think if you were to drop one. Do you like that pot in particular? You're petting it like a cat.

But then, I went on, one doesn't want to feel a painting, even a de Kooning or a Pollack or one of those new lumpy things. That's a dimension missing in paintings.

Your books are like that.

What, missing something.

No no, quite the opposite. What you want is what is behind the business of shaking hands perhaps. A strange custom, when you think about it. Nobody else does that.

I thought it was hugs now, I said, not caring to dispute the assertion.

Just my point. You were going to tell me a story?

I did say so, yes. But I've forgotten it.

Steve gave me one of her practiced suspicious expressions, of which she has a considerable repertoire. This was one of the slitty-eyed sort, with just a hint of something worldly about the corners of the mouth.

I believe, she said, I've heard that English is the only language which permits beginning a sentence with *but*. Have you been taking your medication?

Yes yes, it's just that we got talking and I forgot my story.

Well you'll just have to think of another one, then.

Steve put down her teapot decisively and sat forward, elbows on the table and forearms crossed, waiting with all attention. The light through the shutters made her skin, the pots, everything glow. It's something you miss in the mountains, that light, thick as syrup.

She had made pancakes that morning, her own milkless eggless sugarless gluten-free recipe! Quite delicious, not what you'd think, especially with her bowl of cut-up strawberries. Perhaps this is why the syrup image came to mind. The breakfast thngs were still on the table with everything else, pushed aside along with an untidy refolded newspaper with the sudoku on top, half done.

Your mother freezes watermelon, Steve mused, a leap which might have puzzled some.

And lettuce, I added.

There is a certain comfort in knowing someone else so long that your mother's way with lettuce is a topic of conversation along with syrupy light, zen tea bowls, and the mysterious properties of sin.

Besides, there's this business of peignoirs rather too see-through at times. One fails to notice a mere odd leap of the mind.

Give us a hug, love, I said, reaching for her hand.

You've been watching old English sitcoms up there in the mountains, Steve said, gently chiding me. Her hand was a bit rough from the pottery and the wet clay bothered her arthritic knuckles. The last joint of the index finger on her right hand had a pronounced inward twist. Perhaps that was why when she pointed something out in what I'd said her reference was often a little askew.

But usually right.

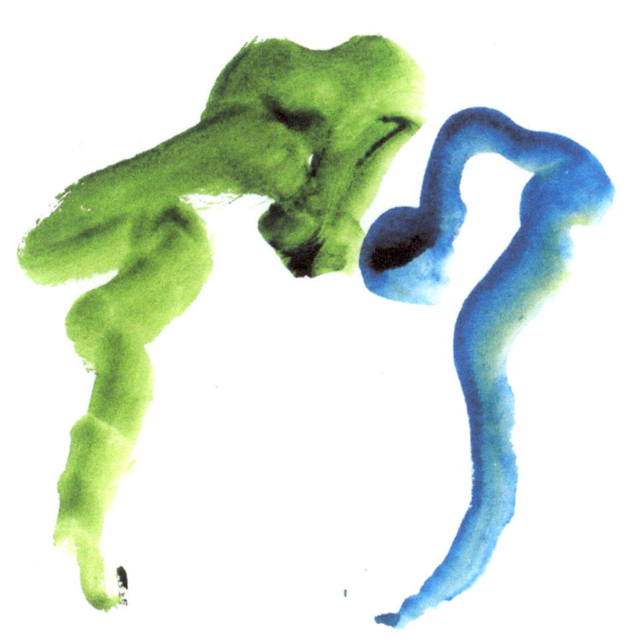